Along the...
Back Roads of Yesterday

By Oris George

Along the Back Roads of Yesterday
by Oris George

www.OrisGeorge.com

©Copyright 2010, by Oris George
Drawings by Shlei of Shlei Original Art
©Puchan/Dreamstime.com
Cover design by Sheri Brady

Published by Distractions Ink
P.O. Box 15971
Rio Rancho, NM 87144

Printed in the United States of America

ISBN 978-0-9827826-9-9

Library of Congress Number: 2010940854

This book is dedicated
to my most precious treasures…
my grandchildren and great grandchildren.

Gratitude

I want to thank my wife, Patsy, for her patience and understanding during the time I have spent putting these stories together.

Without the support, encouragement and contributions of Jan Verhoeff, Danielle Simone, Don Buck and Patricia Dunn, this book would still be an idea in my head.

Table of Contents

Foreward

All writers are not the same.

Throughout this book, *Along the Back Roads of Yesterday*, Oris George takes us to a different, unique reality, not usually found in normal nostalgia. He whisks you away to a time in the not too far past, when life held more simplicity, more family, more fun.

Oris' capacity to tell a story shines through his Mother's cocky rooster sporting a top hat and tuxedo, his ornery billy goat whose life's goal amounts to keeping Oris' little brother, Eddie, trapped in their outhouse and through his buddy Henry, who teaches him much about getting into trouble, about friendship and about life – particularly in the 1940's.

Several years ago I wrote an article about Oris entitled *A Love Affair with Words*. His prolific writing career through books, magazines and newspapers (here and abroad) attests to his lifelong *affair* with words.

But Oris also has a love affair *with life*. No parts of his days are left unturned, no corner unexamined, no idea unexplored, no person in his reach left without their share of his insatiable energy, intelligence and caring.

The emotional and intellectual adventure you will experience through the pages of *Along the Back Roads of Yesterday*, will leave you changed, filled with a different corner of life - life through the war years, life on a hard-working farm, life during a childhood that overflows with an abundance of youthful energy and imagination, and life clothed in the harsh realities of the 1940's.

Enjoy your dance... *Along the Back Roads of Yesterday.*

Danielle Simone
Columnist

Oris George on Red, Circa 1942

The Man at the Side of the Road

"Oris. Getting you to listen to what I'm telling you is like asking a pet mouse to eat a bushel of red apples."

I had asked Mom if I could hitch my mule, Red, to the cart and go for a drive. (Red wasn't really my mule but I claimed him.) He was a small one-eyed aggravating mule Dad let me ride and drive.

Mom's answer didn't make the day any better.

"Bring some wood for the kitchen stove, fill the kitchen water bucket, and take out the trash." I tried not to listen to what she was saying, but my ears wouldn't shut off.

"But—Mom, I want to go now. I'll do those chores when I get back."

"You're not listening to me."

"OKAY. I hear you. You don't have to yell."

"Don't get mouthy with me, young man. I'm not yelling; I'm trying to get you to listen, for once, to what I'm saying."

That hot summer of 1941 is still fresh in my memory.

World War II raged in Europe and Africa. The

3

term, *the Germans*, struck fear into the hearts of me and my eight-year-old friends. When I was riding Red or driving him to the cart, I daydreamed and played like he was a large beautiful horse instead of a one-eyed, contrary red mule. Out by myself, I couldn't hear my parents, grandparents and the neighbors talk about the war.

The water bucket was always empty. The big gray Monarch cook stove was always hungry. The trash basket was always full. I had more important things to do than be bothered with chores.

Mom didn't see it that way.

Hanging the shiny water bucket on the pump spout, I raised the pump handle and poured a little water from a can into the pump to prime it. Water splashed into the bucket as I pumped the handle up and down. With the full bucket in my left hand, I opened the kitchen door, walked to the water bucket stand, and set the bucket by the dipper.

"How many times do you have to be told not to fill that bucket so full? Now look what you've done. You've splashed water all across the floor. Get a rag and wipe up that mess. I've too much to do. I can't be cleaning up after you all the time."

I wiped up the water and started out the door to go get wood.

"And don't slam that door when you go out."

General, Mom's big Buff Orpington rooster,

perched on top of the woodpile, peered down at me with beady eyes. Wearing a black cowboy hat, a blue shirt with a red bandana around his neck, a pair of brown leather chaps, along with yellow cowboy boots and silver spurs, he looked over-dressed—even for a rooster.

He removed a large black cigar from between his pointed chicken lips and said, "You come any closer to this woodpile and I'll give you a lot-of-what-for. This is my yard. I bought this farm from the bank. I don't want a skinny little boy like you messing around and causing trouble."

I went back to the house. "Mom! The rooster is on top of the woodpile and won't let me get wood." Mom came out of the house and shooed that sneaky rooster off the woodpile. (He had shed his clothes. He didn't want Mom to see him dressed up.)

He strutted past me and in a low gravelly voice Mom couldn't hear said, "Next time I see you, I'll peck your eyes out for causing trouble."

Three trips to the woodpile and the wood box was full. (No sign of the bothersome yellow rooster.)

While I was busy carrying in wood, Mom, thinking there wasn't enough for me to do, found more trash. Two trips to the trash barrel and freedom beckoned.

Red didn't want to be caught. He trotted to the south end of the small pasture and waited for me. I put a rope around his neck. No way did he want to wear

5

a bridle. Finally, he lowered his head and let me bridle him. "Come on mule, "I said." Let's go to the barn."

Red stood tied by the barn door while I brushed, combed and harnessed him. I led him to the cart where he stood 'still as a fat turtle on a hot day' while I hooked him between the shaves. "Good mule," I said, and patted him on the neck. "Let's get out of here before Mom finds something else for me to do."

I whistled for Buster, my long-haired brown dog. He jumped into the cart and sat on the seat beside me.

"Git up, Red," I said. "Let's go."

Red was an aggravating mule. One thing he did like to do was pull the cart. He raised his head high and broke into a trot as we left the barnyard. Mom saw us coming and hollered as we drove past the house. "Oris. You stay off the county road and get back here before chore time. Do you hear me?"

"I'll be home in time to chore," I said, and waved as Red picked up the pace.

Grandad and Grandma Fletcher lived down the road from us. Grandma was hanging clothes on the clothes line. She waved.

At the fork in the road, I pulled Red to a stop. Our road turned right and ran along the brow of the hill and over to the reservoir. The other road led to the county road. "Red, which road should we take?" I asked. Mom had told me to stay off the county road, but I could tell that was where he wanted to go. "Okay,

Red. You win."

From our lane, we turned north. Red went at a 'spanking' trot. Buster jumped off the seat and followed along behind the cart.

Red's hooves beat a tattoo on the hard road. The trace chains on the harness jingled a merry tune. The musical sound of those trace chains that day, and the sound of trace chains these many years later remain my favorite sound.

A small flock of red-winged blackbirds arose from the cattails, scolding us for disturbing them.

Buster flushed a large speckled cock pheasant from the weeds along the left side of the road. Mr. Pheasant dropped from sight into a tasseled cornfield.

A lone hawk drifted slowly and effortlessly in the bright blue sky above us.

We rounded the bend. Ahead of us a man walked on the right side of the road. He wore a small brown hat, carried a tall walking staff in his right hand, and had a pack on his back. He stepped off the road and turned to face us. "Good afternoon, young man, I heard you coming. Thought I'd better get out of your way."

I pulled on the lines. "Whoa, Red." He stopped and turned his head to look at the stranger. Buster eased over and sniffed the man's shoes. The stranger reached down and scratched Buster behind the left ear. Buster, acting like he had known the man all his life, lay down on the ground at his feet.

"Where is that red mule taking you on this fine day?"

"I'm going for a drive. What are you doing out here by yourself?"

He stepped to the cart and rested his left hand on the cart wheel. "I'm out to see where I can go."

"That don't sound like fun to me," I said."

"One day I decided to walk to San Francisco. I left New Your City and this is where I am now. I've worn out three pair of shoes. I've seen lots of country and met nice people. I've not met a small boy and a red mule until now.

"What do you eat?" I asked.

"I manage quite well."

"Where do you sleep?"

"At times, along the side of a road or under a bridge. Sometimes in a farmer's barn."

"I'd like to do that. Then, I wouldn't have to take a bath." I thought for a few seconds and said, "My Dad will let you sleep in our barn tonight. It's summer and no mules or cows in the barn at night. It would be nice and quiet."

He smiled as he said, "Well, it sounds good to me." Stepping up into the cart, he placed his pack under the seat and sat down holding the walking staff between his legs. I turned Red around, and we went back towards home. The walking staff, standing straight in the air, looked like a small flagpole,

Red headed back to the barn, trotting faster than when we left. Wherever we went, he always picked up speed on the way home.

"I haven't ridden in a cart since I was a boy about your age. How old are you?"

"I'm almost eight."

"That's a good age. You'll be a grown man soon enough."

Red was in a hurry to get to the barn. It didn't take long to reach our lane. Buster ran on ahead of us. He barked all the way to the house to announce our arrival. Any other time, he'd ride in the cart or follow along behind.

Mom heard Buster's barking and came out of the house. She was standing in the dappled shade of the cottonwood tree, waiting to see what the commotion was all about. Red stopped when I said 'whoa'. (I kept a tight hold on the lines because he wanted to go on to the barn.)

"Mom," I said, "I told this man Dad would let him sleep in the barn tonight, 'cause he'll have to sleep under a bridge if he doesn't find a better place. It's summer, and there are no mules or cows in the barn. He can sleep in the hayloft on fresh hay." (The expression on her face said she didn't think much of the idea.)

"I don't know what to say. My husband isn't here

now. He won't be home until about chore time."

Mr. Thatcher looked at the woodpile and said, "From past experience, I know there is never enough split wood to feed the stoves. I'd be happy to pick up an ax and go to work splitting wood until your husband gets home."

The expression on Mom's face softened. "Okay." She said.

Mr. Thatcher leaned his walking staff against the fence and placed his pack on the ground. Buster plopped down beside it. "Git up, Red," I said. Let's go to the barn and unhitch from this cart."

"Oris, when you get that mule taken care of, come in the house. We're going to have a talk." Mr. Thatcher looked up and winked at me.

On the way back to the house, I saw General Rooster scratching in the dirt at some imaginary tasty morsel. As usual, the silly hens fell for the trick and raced to see what he had discovered, only to be disappointed. I picked up a handful of small pebbles and tossed them at him.

The hens squawked and scattered in different directions. General fluffed up his feathers and glared at me.

Mr. Thatcher chuckled and said, "Looks to me like you and that yellow rooster are having a struggle to see who is boss around here."

"That dumb rooster thinks he's tuff, but he ain't." I

said. "One of these days I'll fix him good.

"Oris, how many times do you have to be told to leave those chickens alone? Quit bothering that man and get in here." Mom held the screen door open.

I slid into a chair at the kitchen table and watched Mom take a clear glass pitcher of cold lemonade form the icebox and fill two glasses. She placed one in front of me and sat down at the table with her glass of lemonade.

"Son, I'm going to tell you something, a secret my grandfather told me when I was about your age. It was a hot day, much like it is today. We were sitting on the front porch watching people go by. Grandfather got up from his wicker chair and went into the house. In a few minutes, he came back, carrying two tall glasses of cold lemonade. "Granddaughter," he said, "I'm going to tell you a secret. Hot summer days and lemonade were made for one another. Now don't you ever forget that. Ya hear?" Mom smiled and sipped her lemonade.

Not knowing where the conversation was going and being a little uneasy, I said, "Mom, you make the best lemonade in the world."

"Thank you," she said, and smiled.

I began to feel uncomfortable.

"Oris, I know you have a kind heart and you never know a stranger. It seems everyone you meet is a friend. That's good in some ways, but in other ways, it's dangerous. Take that man out there chopping wood.

11

He seems like a nice man, a gentleman. It was kind of you to ask him home. But, son, we don't know from where he came, where he is going or where he will be next week. I will not feel safe until your father gets back and talks with him. From now on, do not invite strangers home. I mean it, son. Do not bring strangers home. Do you understand what I'm saying?"

"Yes. Ma'am." I said. "But Mom, he might be hungry, and he will have to sleep under a bridge or in a field or in a ditch. Besides, he liked Red, and Buster likes him lots."

Mom set her lemonade glass on the table. She looked at me and shook her head. "I understand what you are saying, but know this—'that mule and that dog don't know everything'. Now, you run along and get an early start on your chores."

I walked past the woodpile and checked to see if that cranky ol' rooster was anywhere around. He wasn't.

Buster was lying in the shade on the north side of the woodshed watching Mr. Thatcher chop wood. "Come on, Buster," I said. "It'll soon be time to milk. Let's go get them cows." Any other time, he would have bounded ahead of me and raced to the gate where the five yellow Jersey cows waited to be let into the corral. Not this time. He turned his head and looked at me, then at Mr. Thatcher, and decided to stay with Mr. Thatcher.

Mr. Thatcher laughed and said, "Looks like that dog thinks the cows don't need him to help you bring them in today."

The cows were standing at the gate waiting to be let into the corral. I opened the gate. Mable, the boss cow, pushed her way to the front of the line and rushed to be first at the barn door. "I don't know why you're in such a hurry, old cow," I said. "It ain't time to milk yet."

While I was feeding the rabbits their hay, grain and fresh water, Dad and Mr. Thatcher sat on the edge of the water trough and talked.

"Come here, son," Dad called. I walked to the trough and stood in front of him.

"This gentleman tells me you said he could sleep in the barn tonight. Do you think the barn is the best place fer a guest to sleep?"

I looked at the ground and said, "I guess so." Dad and Mr. Thatcher laughed.

"Son, I'll tell ya what we're gonna do. Mr. Thatcher's gonna help with chores. He said he ain't milked a cow in twenty years. You let the cows in the barn. I'll git another milk bucket fer Mr. Thatcher, and we'll see if he still knows how ta milk a Jersey cow. After chores, we'll go ta the house and have one o' your mother's good suppers. This man is gonna sleep in the spare bedroom tonight. Tomorrow I'll drive him ta town so he can git some things he needs ta continue his trip.

13

That sound okay ta you?"

"Yes, sir." I said.

Mr. Thatcher milked two cows. The streams of milk beat a tattoo on the bottom of the bucket and told us he still knew how to milk a cow.

We finished chores.

When we got to the house, Mom had the table set with fried chicken, fresh baked buttermilk biscuits, mashed potatoes, green beans and roasting ears from her garden, and a silver pitcher of cold milk.

"Mrs. Fletcher, I haven't had a meal like this in years. Thank you so much."

For dessert, Mom had baked a blueberry cobbler. She served it with thick cream.

For once, my two younger brothers were quiet during supper.

When supper was finished, dishes were pushed to the middle of the table. The folks and Mr. Thatcher talked for a long time. Mom told me to get ready for bed.

"Goodnight, Mom. Goodnight, Dad. Goodnight, Mr. Thatcher." I said.

"I hope you have a gentle sleep tonight young man, and thank you for bringing me to your home."

My bedroom was upstairs over the kitchen. A grate in the floor allowed warm air from the kitchen to heat my room in the winter. After I was ready for bed, I crawled over to the grate and listened to the conversation.

Mr. Thatcher told my parents about his son going off to war. One afternoon two Army officers came to his door and told him his son had been killed in action in Germany.

"My son, Anthony, was all I had. His mother had been dead for seven years. My heart was broken. I didn't know what to do. I thought I'd die. The third of February I woke up, decided to close up the house, and walk to San Francisco. I'd always wanted to see California. I put boards over every window and gave the keys to my good neighbor, Augustus Chapo, to look after things until I got back."

"We're sorry for you loss. " Mom said. "I can't imagine what it would be like to lose a child."

"This walking adventure has been good for me. I've had a lot of time to think and remember the love, good times, and the sound of laughter that filled our home. Yes, walking has been good for me."

I felt tired and worn out. I wasn't sure I wanted to hear more, but I didn't want to miss any of what he was saying.

"Do you have any idea how long it will take you to reach San Francisco?" Dad asked.

"No, sir. I don't have any idea at all. One thing for sure, I enjoy walking and I've met some wonderful people—people like you folks who are kind and understanding."

The talk in the kitchen turned to war.

I didn't understand the war or anything about it. The discussion scared me. I crawled back to my bed and pulled the covers over my head to block the sounds of war that were echoing in my mind. The news reel at the movies on Saturday afternoon showed soldiers, sailors, fires, long lines of people evacuating their towns and homes, bombs, gunfire, the scream of dive bombers, fighter planes, and battleships.

I tossed and turned, very much afraid, until sleep turned off the frightening pictures and sounds rampaging through my head.

The sound of tap, tap, tap woke me from a groggy sleep. Mom's broom was tapping the ceiling in the kitchen, telling me it was time to get up. "I'm coming," I said, even thought I wasn't fully awake.

The folks and Mr. Thatcher were sitting at the kitchen table having their first cup of coffee for the day.

"Son," Dad said, "Mr. Thatcher wants ta help with the chores this mornin' so apply the seat o' yer pants ta that chair and have a glass o' milk ta start yer day."

Again, Mr. Thatcher enjoyed milking two cows. He helped me feed the calves and the pigs. We put the mules in the barn so they would be there when Grandad came to get them. He was going to haul some gravel for the driveway. Next, we drove the cows down the lane to pasture. Buster nipped at Daisy's heels to hurry her along—she was always the last cow in line. Contrary Mable led the herd, most often in the wrong direction, but this day she followed the lane without making a fuss.

I closed the gate.

We watched the five Jersey cows fan out across the pasture and begin grazing the fresh green grass. Mable stuck her nose in the air and headed for greener pastures, but the fence got in her way. She settled for the greenest blades furtherest from the lane.

Mr. Thatcher placed his left hand on my right shoulder and said, "When you are grown and have been gone from home for many years, once in a while, your memory will remind you of how peaceful it was when you took the cows down this lane in the morning and brought them back in the evening. I know, because I've been there.

"Hey, you two," Dad called. "Are you gonna take all day? Let's head fer the house and breakfast."

After a breakfast of fried eggs, sausage, gravy and biscuits with coffee black enough to stand alone without a cup, Mom wrapped a lunch in newspaper tied up with string from one of the many balls of white string around our house. She handed it to Mr. Thatcher. "Here's a little lunch for you later today."

Mr. Thatcher removed his hat and held it in his left hand. "Thank you, Mrs. Fletcher, for your kindness and hospitality and the delicious food. You are an excellent cook. Those were the tenderest biscuits I've had in many miles. I shall never forget my visit here."

Dad parked his old beat-up black Ford pickup by the porch steps. "Git in you two, and we'll run inta town so this man can git some things he needs."

Mr. Thatcher placed his pack and walking stick in the back of the pickup. He opened the door and said, "Oris, let me sit in the middle. I know young boys like to ride shotgun and not be crowded between two grown-ups."

We waited in the pickup while Mr. Thatcher went into the Red and White grocery store to buy a few items. Then Dad drove east down the road. He parked the pickup on the right side of the road and the three of us got out.

Mr. Thatcher extended his right hand to Dad and said, "Thank you, Mr. Fletcher, for your kindness and hospitality. I shall never forget you and your family."

My eyes were holding back a rush of tears.

Mr. Thatcher put his right hand on my shoulder, looked into my eyes and said, "Young man, thank you for finding me along the side of the road and taking me to your home. You've made my heart happy. I'll remember you, your red mule, your dog, Buster, and General, the yellow rooster, for as long as God lets me stay on this earth." He shouldered his pack and with his walking staff in his right hand, he started down the road. Dad and I watched this gentle-hearted man walk away.

When Mr. Thatcher reached the bend in the road, he turned. Raising his walking staff in a farewell gesture, he walked around the bend and out of sight.

Seven months later, the mailman left a letter for me in our mailbox. The letter read, "Oris, I am in San Francisco. Your friend, Antone Thatcher."

The years traveled on, as years do. Once in a while I'd get a short note from Mr. Thatcher. The notes usually were signed, "Your friend, Antone Thatcher, the man from the side of the road."

Sixty-some years later, in the corner by my desk, stands my walking staff. Often, I look at it and think of 'the man by the side of the road'.

Ol' Billy

"Now, mind your manners and be polite. Be sure and say 'thank you' and 'please.' And, for heaven's sake, if your nose starts to drip, use your hanky instead of your shirt sleeve!" Those were my mother's parting instructions that summer 60 some years ago when she dropped me off in front of my friend Henry's house. She then drove away in her 1927 Whippet. Henry and I were six years old, almost seven.

That day, in the summer of 1940, was the beginning of many wonderful and fun-filled times Henry and I shared over the years to come. (Today, at the tender age of 73, I still worry that my 100-year old mother will discover some of the things Henry and I did while we terrorized the community as two energetic boys looking for adventure.)

Two events stand out in my mind about that first time I stayed overnight with Henry. I was worried about how to use the bathroom. (We had outdoor plumbing at our house.) The second was Mort and ol' Billy. After about an hour, I was introduced to the 'scary' indoor facilities and put that fear behind me. (Young boys worry about those new kinds of challenges.)

"You want to go see ol' Billy?" Henry asked.

"Sure," I said. (That was one dumb question.)

Ol' Billy was a white donkey which belonged to Mort Singer. Everyone knew Mort and ol' Billy. That is, everyone but me. I lived out in the country and didn't know much about what went on in town.

Ol' Billy pulled a wobbly-wheeled cart that served as Mort's only means of transportation. During the spring and summer, Mort and ol' Billy plowed and cultivated gardens around town. That white donkey pulled a six-inch walking plow with as much pride as a magnificent dappled-grey Percheron draft horse hitched to a fancy wagon. Each Saturday morning, come rain or shine, found Mort and his dependable donkey hauling trash for a few regular customers.

Henry's father told us we would find Mort down by the river cutting grass. He said Mort had a hand scythe and was cutting grass to cure. That's how and where he acquired hay for ol' Billy.

We found Mort swinging a scythe with the grace and timing of a well-oiled machine. "What you two hellions adoin' down here abotherin' me for?"

Henry, even at that early age, was not at a loss for words. "We wanna see ol' Billy."

"Git-outta-here and don't come abotherin' ah man when he's aworkin'!"

We found ol' Billy tied to the back end of the cart. With his long ears drooping and his eyes closed, he was at peace with the world. We walked over to pet him, which was a big mistake! Mort saw us and yelled, "Ya bothersome little brats. Gittaway from thet thar donkey!"

We moseyed on down to the river. I spied a magpie nest in a twisted cottonwood tree just begging us to investigate. We climbed the tree and peered into the nest. Two magpie chicks chirped at us. (Henry responded by telling them we were not their mother.) We put them in our caps and started down the tree.

Mort hollered, "What you idiot boys adoin' with them thar magpies in yer caps fer?" He stood at the foot of the tree glaring up at us.

We dropped to the ground. Henry looked at Mort and said, "We're takin' 'em home so we can teach'em to talk."

"You boys set down thar by thet tree and I'm agonna tell ya some things 'bout magpies." (Henry rolled his eyes at me.)

"Magpies am nasty birds. They carry more'n one of them bad diseases. They got more lice on 'em than 91 coyotes. They eat dead stuff, like rabbits which been kill'd on the road, an' dead cows, an' chicken guts. If'n a cow or horse gets caught in ah fence, them magpie birds'll pick their eyes out. Ya boys leave them magpies be or ya'll get a bad disease, and grow a big

23

ugly wart on the end of yer noses!" (When I got home that night I scrubbed my nose until it was red.)

As summers do (when boys are young), time drifted along with no place to go. Every once in a while we saw Mort. We considered him our idol. My mother didn't think him a good example for two young boys. She said he drank too much whiskey. She knew his overalls had never seen the inside of a washing machine. And, he had an ongoing feud with soap.

One warm Saturday night, late in the summer, Mort had too much whiskey and ended up sleeping on a bench in the park. Come morning, Frankie Gadberry, a local horse trader and an all-around lout, offered Mort five dollars for ol' Billy. Mort, in his bleary state, took the five dollars. Later, when he realized he had sold his faithful donkey, he was devastated. That old white donkey meant the world to him.

Little Man

This morning, Punky, my wife of fifty-four years, suggested I sort through a box of 'stuff' taking up space on the top shelf in the hall closet. (The translation of that suggestion meant, "get rid of that junk or I'll throw it out.") In that dusty old shoe box, I found a cracked and yellowed picture of Homer.

As I looked at the picture, the years washed away and again I could hear, "What is that stinking goat doing in my kitchen?" Mom grabbed a broom and went after my billy goat, Homer. With the rage of a Mongolian Warrior, she convinced him he should exit the kitchen. Exit he did, right through the bottom half of the screen door. With her trusty broom, she impressed on me the idea that she would not tolerate my bringing a goat that smelled like a combination of skunk and onions into her kitchen.

"If I catch that foul-smelling goat anywhere near this house again, he will wish he had never been born," Mom said. "Young man, if you know what is good for you, you will keep that mangy goat penned up. I don't want to see him running loose around this farm anymore. Do you hear me!?"

"Okay! Okay! Okay! I hear you."

"Oris. Don't you get smart with me."

I darted out the screen door and hot-footed it around the corner of the house to get away from Mom's nagging and ran smack-dab into Homer. I fell, nose down on my face.

"Oris!" Mom screeched. I scrambled to my feet and followed Homer. Homer lit out for the safety of the machine shed. I headed for the barn. Neither of us wanted to be anywhere near Mom and her broom.

A year before this incident, Tex Duggan, a neighbor, gave me a little brown billy goat. I named him Homer after a friend in my third grade class. Homer thought he was a dog. He went everywhere I went. Now, as a full-grown goat, he still followed me every chance he got. That's how he happened to be in Mom's kitchen that hot summer July afternoon of 1940.

I ran into the barn and shut the door. I could hear Mom calling. "Oris. Get back here right now!"

At seven years old, I already had learned not to answer Mom's calling. If she was busy and couldn't see me, she soon forgot.

"What's goin' on, boy?" Dad asked. He was standing by the grain box with a bucket of oats in his right hand.

"Nothing." I said. Panic hit me. If he heard Mom calling me, he'd tell me to go back to the house.

"If you ain't doin' nothin', come help me catch Pete and Pattie. Them mules don't see the need ta pull the mower taday."

I held the bucket of oats. Pete stuck his nose in the bucket. Dad put a halter on him and led him into the barn. Pattie followed.

"Can I ride Red over to Grandad's this morning?" Red was a one-eyed red mule I rode. I wanted a donkey, but Dad said Red had a lot to teach me before I could have a donkey.

"It's okay with me. You'd best ask yer mother if it's alright with her."

Asking Mom if I could ride over to Grandad Fletcher's wasn't a good idea. She'd still be angry with Homer and me.

"I think I'll just ride over to the pond and back. Is that okay?"

"Sure. Be careful and don't go gittin' yerself lost." Dad laughed. He harnessed Pete and Patti and went to mow hay in the field south of the barn.

"M-aw-aw-aw-M-aw-aw-aw! Eddie, my little brother, was calling for Mom. When he called like that, I knew he was in the outdoor toilet and needed help. The help he most often needed was for Mom or someone to run Homer away from the toilet door. If Homer saw Eddie go to the toilet, he'd stand in front

27

of the door and butt it to keep Eddie from coming out. Eddie was afraid of Homer, and Homer seemed to know it.

I peered around the corner of the chicken house. Mom, with her broom in hand, headed for the toilet to rescue Eddie. No sign of Homer anywhere. Eddie must have had a false alarm.

Red had other ideas and didn't want to be caught. He was a greedy mule and always took the ear of corn I offered. Then, I'd snap the lead rope into his halter ring.

I rode over to the pond, skipped flat rocks across the smooth water, and threw rocks at red-winged black birds.

When I got back to the house, I caught Homer and shut him in his pen. Mom had forgotten about my taking him into the kitchen.

After chores were done, supper over, and dishes washed and put in the cupboard, Mom, Dad, and we three boys sat on the porch and put the day to rest to the tune of homemade strawberry ice cream.

Morning arrived and found Mom standing at the foot of the stairs hollering up at me. "Oris. Time to get up. Your father's already gone to the barn. He needs you to help move the big calves into another pen. Hurry it up!"

Chores were finished. Breakfast was a friendly memory. The day awaited. Like she did with every perfect day, Mom ruined this one. "Oris, before you go ride that red mule, I want you to help in the garden." (The word 'garden' always sent chills along my backbone.) "When you get the weeds out of the onions, pull the weeds along the south fence. Then hoe the beets."

"Okay, Mom," I said. "Then can I ride Red over to Grandad Fletcher's?"

"Yes, but not until you're done with the weeds."

I'd been slaving in the garden for about an hour. "Why do I hafta be here with you dumb weeds? There's more to life than hoein' you stupid weeds. I've better things to do than be out here sweatin' in the sun with you dumb weeds."

I saw Eddie go down the path to the toilet. He went inside and shut the door. Eddie thought he was safe. Homer was locked in his pen.

At the age of seven years, I once in a while had a good idea. Homer, standing at his gate, looked bored. He needed something to do. The toilet door, begging for Homer to butt it a few times and keep Eddie inside, appealed to my helpful nature. I leaned the hoe against the fence and crawled under the bottom rail. Homer, anticipating my letting him out, began trotting back and forth in his pen. I opened the gate. Homer lowered his head and went for the toilet door. BANG! His horns hit the door! He backed off a little distance. BANG! He hit the door again.

Ma-aw-aw-Ma-aw-aw! Eddie issued his clarion call for help. Homer heard the screen door slam. Past experience had taught him he'd better git-gone-and-fast. He left for the safety of the machine shed. Mom opened the toilet door. Eddie, tears running down his ruddy cheeks said, "Homer wouldn't let me out."

"I told Oris to keep that goat penned up and he'd better do it."

I smiled and finished weeding the garden. I caught Homer and put him in his pen, then rode over to Grandad Fletcher's.

Red never got in a hurry going away from home. A kick in the ribs to encourage him to move faster didn't make a shake-of-salt difference. He switched his ratty-looking tail and maintained the same slow plod.

Grandad saw us coming and opened the gate. "Hey there, you one-eyed red mule. Where ya goin' with this here pip-squeak of a boy?"

"I'm not a pip-squeak."

"Well. Ya don't look like Roy Rogers, and that red mule don't look ta me like Trigger. So that makes ya a pip-squeak."

Grandad closed the gate. I slid off Red and we walked up the lane to the barn.

"Tie that fire-eatin' mule to the fence and let's go ta the house and see if yer grandmother has some cold lemonade left in the icebox."

"What are you two loafers doing coming into

my kitchen this time of day?" Grandma smiled and pinched my left cheek. I loved my grandmother but didn't like the way she pinched my cheek every time she got a chance.

Grandad looked at me and smiled his crooked smile. "This boy arrived on his high-spirited, high-steppin' red mule. I could tell that mule 'bout got the best o' him. I think a glass o' cold lemonade is what he needs after that f-a-s-t ride."

"Now, Grandad," Grandma said. "That red mule doesn't move fast enough to shake the lice off if he was in a wind storm. I think it's you who wants the lemonade." She poured two glasses of cold lemonade.

"Thanks, Grandma. This sure is good stuff."

Grandad scratched the left side of his nose. "What's goin' on over ta yer place taday?" He asked.

"Nuthin' much. Dad's rakin' hay. Mom's cannin' beans. Ralph is ridin' his bike up and down the lane. Homer kept Eddie in the toilet for a little bit." I laughed.

Grandma attached a serious look to her face and said, "One of these days that goat is going to hurt Eddie. You should keep him penned up."

"Naw. He's not gonna hurt Eddie." I grinned. Grandad looked at me. I thought I saw a slight twitch at the left corner of his mouth. No doubt about it, his eyes were laughing. I had another glass of lemonade while I visited with Grandma and Grandad.

31

"I guess I'd better go on home. I don't want to be late doin' chores. Thanks for the lemonade, Grandma."

I untied Red. Grandad walked with me to the gate. He gave me a leg-up on Red and closed the gate behind us. "See you later, Grandad." I heeled Red. He started toward home at a fast walk. He was in a hurry to get there.

I fed the calves and helped Dad milk the cows. We finished up the evening chores and went to the house.

"Oris. Wash your hands and change into a clean shirt before we eat supper," Mom said.

For supper, Mom had fixed fried chicken, mashed potatoes, green beans fresh from her garden and rhubarb pie. The conversation around the table died down. Mom started in on me about Homer.

"If you don't keep that fool goat penned up, you'll have to get rid of him. Do you understand me? I've got other things to do besides chase him away from the toilet door every time Eddie is in there."

I liked Homer and didn't want to get rid of him.

Ralphie looked at Mom and said, "I saw Oris let Homer out of his pen when Eddie went to the toilet. Homer made straight for the toilet door, and Oris was laughing. He looked at me with a 'smirk' on his face that made me want to punch him."

Mom laid her fork on the edge of her plate. She looked across the table at me and said, "Knowing Eddie was in the toilet, you turned that goat loose on purpose?" I looked down at my plate. "Look at me when I'm talking to you."

"Yes, Homer slipped out when I opened the gate. I'll keep him penned up all the time. He won't cause any more trouble. I'll even tie him on a chain if I have to. PLEASE, Mom, don't make me get rid of him. I'll take good care of him so he won't bother Eddie."

Before Mom could say anything, Dad said, "Son. That goat has turned out to be a real pest 'round here. If you keep 'im penned up and take care of 'im you can keep 'im. The first time he gits out and causes trouble, you'll have ta git rid of 'im. Is that understood?

"Yes, sir." I said.

Mom wanted to say something, but changed her mind and started clearing the table.

Dad pushed his empty plate to the center of the table and looked at me. "Son," he said. "We're not gonna have that goat causin' problems. Like I said, you keep 'im penned up and out o' trouble and ya can keep 'im.' You understand me?"

I looked down at my plate and said, "Yes, sir."

Mom exploded. "How many times do you have to be told not to look at your plate when someone is talking to you!" She put six dirty glasses on the counter.

I slid off my chair and slunk out the kitchen door.

Ralph followed me out to the woodpile. "You're gonna hav'ta git rid of Homer, and I'm glad. Mother says Homer has been a problem from day one." I almost hit him but thought better of it. Hitting him would get me in deeper trouble with Mom.

Ralph went back into the house. I sat on the chopping block trying to figure out what to do. Biggs stood in front of me wagging his tail. He licked me square in the face. "Git outta here, you darn dog." He licked me again.

Somehow, I had to get on Mom's good side. It came to me! She spent half her time complaining about the wood box by the kitchen stove being empty. She harped at me every day to keep wood in the box.

I picked up an armload of firewood and went back into the kitchen to fill the wood box. The Home Comfort cookstove, a grey monster, was always hungry. I don't know how many times a day Mom would say, "Oris. Fill the wood box." After supper, she'd say, "Oris. Fill the wood box." If I went in the house for a drink of water, she'd say, "Oris. Fill the wood box." There was no doubt in my handsome mind that that grey monster ate more wood than any other two wood-burning cookstoves in the county.

"It's about time you got wood in here. Get ready for bed. There are clean socks and jeans folded and ready to take up to your room. Don't pile them on the dresser. Put the socks in the sock drawer and hang the jeans on hangers. Dirty clothes are scattered all over up there. Pick them up and put them in the basket. What are you doing? Trying to live like a pig in that room?"

With clean clothes crammed under my left arm, I trudged up the stairs and put them on the chest of drawers (instead of the dresser).

It didn't take long to pick up dirty clothes and pile them in the clothes basket. The basket overflowed. I stepped on them and mashed them down enough so they wouldn't spill over on the floor.

I got into my pajamas and lit the kerosene lamp at the head of my bed. Last Saturday, Henry and I traded comic books. I now had a new Captain Marvel I wanted to read. I was about ready to hop into bed when I heard Mom and Dad talking. I crawled across the floor to the heat grill in the floor at the far side of my room. In the winter, it let the heat from the kitchen warm my room. At anytime, I could listen to what was going on in the kitchen.

Mom said something I couldn't hear. She must have been on the other side of the kitchen, too far away for me to hear.

Dad chuckled, "He sure sets store by that goat."

"Yes, he does. However, that makes no difference. He either cares for that goat and keeps him out of trouble or down the road that stinking thing goes. No ifs-ands-or-buts about it."

Dad chuckled again, "Homer has a better nose than most Bloodhounds. The other day Oris went up ta the well. That goat started looking for 'im. You'da laughed." He paused. I heard him slap his knee.

"Homer raced around the machine shed and over ta the orchard looking fer that kid. All at once, he headed straight up the path ta the well."

"I'm not the least bit interested in how smart that goat is."

"I know yer not. I feel the same way 'bout 'im most o' the time. But there are times I kinda enjoy 'im," Dad said. "Wednesday, I watched the four of 'em, Oris riding Red, Homer and the dog trailing along behind. The four o' 'em didn't have a care in the world. My heart kinda warmed watchin' 'em."

The screen door hinges squeaked. Dad went outside to smoke his last cigarette of the day.

I crawled into bed, pulled the covers up to my waist, and read about Captain Marvel and his new adventure. The second step on the stairs groaned. Mom was on her way up. I shut my eyes and played like I was asleep. She tip-toed over to the bed and brushed a soft kiss on my forehead and said, "Sleep well, little man." She blew out the lamp and went back down the stairs.

All too soon, the cranky red rooster crowed, telling the world it was time to be up and about. Daylight hadn't yet thought about creeping over the mountain to the east. Relaxing in bed before full daylight was my favorite activity of the day. The cook stove lid clattered as Mom lifted it and set it to the back of the stove The lid clattered again when she put it back in place. I could hear the snap of cedar wood catching fire. Soon the clamoring smell of fresh brewed coffee climbed up through the grate in the floor. (One of the most comforting sounds I remember as a kid at home was listening to Mom build a fire in the cook stove.)

From the foot of the stairs, Mom called. "Oris. It's time to get up."

"Okay, Mom."

I dragged out of bed, dressed, and went to the barn.

Leaning over the fence, I dumped a full bucket of yellow corn in the trough for the squealing pigs. "Come on, pigs, "I said. "Quit squealing and shoving and get your front feet out of the trough."

Dad finished milking Daisy, his favorite yellow Jersey cow, while I fed the calves and put fresh water in the rabbits' drinking bowls.

On the way to the house for breakfast, Dad asked, "How you an' ol' Red gittin' along."

"Okay. He sure makes me tired, the way he walks so slow and don't want to go where I want him to half the time. He's hard to catch and kinda sulky sometimes. When can I get a donkey?"

"One of these fine days ya can git a donkey. Fer now, Red still has a lot ta teach ya." Dad placed his calloused right hand on my left shoulder as we walked to the house.

Mom, with a white dish towel thrown over her left shoulder, was standing at the stove frying ham and eggs.

"Mother! Oris touched me," Ralph said.

"Mamma. Oris pushed me," Eddie said. He started to whimper.

"Charles. I've got my hands full trying to get breakfast on the table. Will you do something with these kids?"

"Okay, boys. That's enough. All three o' ya wash yer hands an' settle down," he said. "Yer mother's gone ta a lot a trouble ta fix breakfast. Any more fightin' and all three o' ya'ill find yerselves goin' without breakfast."

"Mamma. Oris stuck his tongue out at me." Ralph said. "I hope Homer dies today or gets shot in the head."

"Another word out o' anyone o' ya and ya' all three'ill be in big trouble. Ya hear that?" Dad said. "Now stop yer fussin' an' eat."

Halfway through breakfast, Mom said, "I'm going to take the eggs and cream into town this morning. Ralph, you and Eddie change into clean shirts. I don't want Aunt Maude seeing you looking like two war orphans."

"Mom, can I go, too?" I asked.

"No. You need to stay home and help your father."

When Dad and I got to the shop, he handed me a small bucket of nails of various sizes and lengths. He said, "Son, sort these nails. Put the big ones in that red coffee can and the little ones in a small can. While ya do that, I'll harness Pete and Patti. Yer granddad's comin' by to git 'em. He's gonna haul some fence posts this mornin'."

I heard Grandad's car stop in front of the shop and went out to meet him.

"Hello there, Pip-squeak," Grandad said. "What's a little boy like you doin' on a fine day like this?" He smiled and tousled my hair.

"I'm not a pip-squeak!"

"That bein' the case then, how 'bout helpin' me hitch them mules ta the green wagon?"

On the way to the barn, we passed Homer. Locked inside his pen, he didn't look very happy. "Good lookin' billy goat ya got there," Grandad said. "It appears Eddie will be safe in the toilet taday."

The day ended on a soft note. Supper was a pleasant memory, and Mom read to us a chapter from the book, *Billy Whiskers*.

The next thing I knew, the know-it-all rooster announced to the world that lazy people should be out of bed. I dressed and went to the barn and had most of my chores done before Dad arrived to do his chores. "Well, boy, what ya doin' up so early?".

"I want to ride Red over to Grandad's this morning after breakfast, if that's okay. Mom's going to town again today. Grandad wants me to help string some fence wire."

For once in their 'sheltered' lives, Ralph and Eddie ate breakfast without chattering like two magpies on the woodpile.

"Charles," Mom said. "I'm going to hang a load of sheets on the line to dry before I go to town. If it looks like rain, will you bring them in so they won't get wet?"

"I can do that. That is if'n ya'll bring me a carton of Lucky Strikes."

I enjoyed helping Granddad fix fence.

Grandma had apple pie for dessert at dinner.

It was chore time when I got home. Something wasn't right. Mom's car was parked under the cottonwood tree instead of by the back door.

Ralph came running around the corner of the house. "Oris. Momma said she's gonna shoot Homer and you and Daddy, too. You're not so big and smart after all."

Mom came to the screen door. In a very soft, quiet voice she said, "Oris, you go to the barn, get your father, and bring him to the house, right now."

"Why?" I asked.

In the same soft, quiet voice, she said, "Never you mind. Just bring him to the house like I asked."

I ran to the barn. Dad was fixing to start chores. "Dad. Mom wants you to come to the house right now."

"What's wrong?"

"I don't know. She sounded awful quiet."

Dad walked so fast I had to run to keep up with

him.

When we got to the house, in the same soft and quiet voice, Mom said, "Charles. I don't ask for much. I care for my family the best way I know how. All I ask is for all of you to meet me halfway in what I do around here."

Dad stood as still as a cedar fence post. For once, he wasn't smiling.

"I hung a load of sheets on the line before I went to town this morning. When I got home, what did I find? Somehow, that goat got out of his pen. I found three sheets ripped to shreds. That sweet billy goat, everyone likes so much, with his horns, had ripped those sheets to ribbons."

Dad started to say something. Mom cut him off.

"Charles. That's not all." She looked at me, her voice still soft and quiet, she continued. "I parked the car under the cottonwood tree because I had the back seat full of groceries and didn't want them to get hot."

Again, Dad started to say something. In that soft voice, she said, "Let me finish. I noticed the sheets in shreds and went to the clothesline to get them. I came around the corner of the house with an arm load of ripped sheets. What did I see? That sw-e-e-t and lovable goat dancing around on top of the car—his sharp hooves punching holes in the cloth top of my car."

Once again, Dad started to say something. Again,

41

she cut him off.

"Charles, Oris. One of you shoots that goat or I will." She folded her arms across her chest and burst into tears.

I had never seen my mother cry. I started to cry. Dad hugged her, and said, "Okay. That goat's gone from here. Oris, you find him and chain him in his pen."

I found Homer in the orchard, standing under an apple tree chewing his cud. I led him back to his pen, snapped a chain to his collar, and tied it to a post. I shut the gate and went to do my chores. No way did I want to face Mom and Dad.

When Dad finished his chores, he said, "Son. Apply the seat of your pants to that box and let me tell ya somethin'."

Before Dad could say a word, I said, "Dad, I'm sorry Homer got out and messed things up."

" 'Sorry' don't cut it, son."

"I know, Dad," I said. "Does this mean I hafta sell Homer?"

"Yes." He said. "Now listen here ta me. When yer mother was fourteen years old, she started pluckin' down from her mamma's geese. She plucked them geese and saved money 'til she had enough ta buy a new car. She paid $421 fer that new Whippet in 1927."

Dad didn't say anything for a few minutes.

"It'll cost better 'n $50 ta fix that cloth roof on yer

mother's car. That's $50 more 'n we have."

I didn't eat supper that night. I went to the barn and sat on a bale of hay in front of Pete's stall. I put my elbows on my knees and my head between my hands and cried. Homer had got himself in a big mess. No doubt about it, Dad would sell him.

The barn door opened, and Dad walked in. "Son," he said. "Homer has outlived his usefulness 'round here. Your mother'n me 'ave decided it's time you 'n him parted company. Come Saturday, I'm gonna sell him at the auction." He patted me on the left shoulder and said, "Come on ta the house." Then, he went back outside.

I waited until the kitchen was dark and slipped upstairs to my room. I flopped across the foot of the bed and sobbed some more. After a bit, I lit the lamp and got ready for bed.

I heard the second stair step squeak and knew Mom was coming upstairs. I pulled covers up to my waist. She stood at the foot of the bed and looked at me. Not saying a word, she just stood there and looked at me.

I covered my eyes with my right hand.

"Oris," she said. "I know you don't want to part with Homer. Sometimes we have to do things we don't want to." She moved my hand away from my eyes and wiped away the tears.

I wanted to tell her how sorry I was for not keeping Homer locked up, but knew the tears would start again.

"Just because you have to get rid of Homer," she said, "babies won't die in their sleep, the sun won't stop coming up, and old women and kids won't die."

A sob escaped my lips.

Mom softened the blow of having to sell Homer by saying, "You have been wanting a donkey for a long time now. Your father and I have decided you can take the money you get for Homer and buy a donkey."

She leaned over and kissed my forehead and said, "I love you, son. Sleep safe, little man."

She blew out the lamp and went back down stairs.

Ol' Sam, a Mule

"Charles, if you had a lick of sense, you'd have sold that cussed mule years ago. Here it is, the middle of haying season. Now, you're going to be laid up for a while," Mom said. Her skirts snapped as she left the room.

After sixty-some years, those were words my memory returned to me this morning.

I was seven years old that muggy summer of 1940.

Dad had a span of big black mules he called Sam and Joe. They were out of black Percheron mares, sired by a grandson of the famous Mammoth Jack, Kansas Chief. Those mares, Kit and Kate, weighed 2,000 pounds each and stood 17 hh—68 inches.

Ol' Sam did a bang-up job of making life miserable for everyone on the ranch. He was hard to catch. Every dog, man or kid that came close to him learned to avoid his heels, or run the risk of being kicked clear into the middle of the next county. When you entered his stall, you had to watch, be careful, or he'd crowd you against the wall.

Every time Dad walked down the alley behind the stalls, ol' Sam kicked at him. Dad would jump out of the way. (Grandad Fletcher said that's how Sam taught Dad to dance.)

Dad was the only one who liked Sam.

My job was to muck out Sam and Joe's stalls. Sam's stall was the first one in a line of six. Sam never kicked at me like he did Dad. He'd just stick his left rear foot out and shake it at me. I didn't trust him and he knew it.

Late one sizzling July evening as Dad and I were cleaning stalls, ol' Sam did his usual 'kick-at-Dad' thing.

"I've had enough of that blasted mule kickin' at me!" Dad said. "I'm gonna teach that 'bugger' a thing-or-two!" He kicked Sam. Sam kicked at Dad. Dad kicked Sam. Sam kicked and connected with Dad's left kneecap. Dad was laid up for a month. All he did during the rest of haying season was boss the job. He walked with a lop-sided limp for the rest of his life.

I could never figure how Sam knew when to stick that foot out and shake it at me.

One evening during chore time, I took a break and sat on a bale of straw in the feed alley. I looked at Sam's stall, and spied a knothole at the end of the manger. A big, soft, brown eye peered at me. I got up off the straw bale and started down the alley behind Sam. As usual, ol' Sam played his game and shook his foot at me.

The next day I nailed a tin can lid over the hole. Ol' Sam never shook his foot at me again.

Mule-Apples!

The summer of 1941 I was seven years old, going on eight. In my mind, I was a man-full-grown, and could do anything. Heck! Like my dad, I could spit five feet and cuss the cat at the same time. I knew better than to let Mom catch me cussing. (She didn't understand man things.)

"Oris. You eat everything on your plate! Some little kid in Germany would like to have what you waste." (So far as I was concerned, she could send my share of spinach and okra to Germany.)

"Okay, Mom. Why don't the other kids have to clean up their plates?" Ralph was five and Eddy three. They never had to clean their plates. (I figured Mom didn't nag them because there was no food left to clean up—it was on their faces, clothes, the table and the floor.)

"Never you mind about the other kids. Hurry up and finish eating. It's Friday night. I need help with the eggs." (G-r-r-r! I'd rather take a beating than help with the dumb eggs!)

Mom's flock of contented Rhode Island Red hens were good layers. They laid large brown eggs. Every Friday night after the barn chores were finished and the supper dishes washed and put away, Mom sorted, candled, and crated the eggs. Come Saturday morning, she harnessed and hitched Sally, her favorite mule, to the Studebaker cart and drove the five miles to Mrs. Cathcart's. Mrs. Cathcart, our neighbor lady and a friend of Mom's, had a flock of flighty White Leghorn hens that laid large white eggs. Mom and Mrs. Cathcart took turns taking the eggs to town. That way neither one 'wasted' a Saturday every week. The feed store bought eggs from local small farmers and sold them to a distributor which had an outlet for them. The man at the feed store paid cash for Mom's eggs. He applied Mrs. Cathcart's egg credit to her feed bill.

Heck! I was almost eight years old and knew for sure-and-certain I could drive a mule to take eggs to Cathcarts'. All summer, I pestered Mom to ask Dad if he thought I was old enough to make the drive alone. I gave up on Mom's asking and decided to ask him myself.

As I finished the last of my apple pie, Dad lit the kerosene lamp and placed it in the middle of the kitchen table. I looked up at him. "Dad, ain't I old enough ta take the eggs ta Cathcarts?"

With his calloused right hand, he tossled my hair and said, "I think it's about time ya took on some additional responsibility 'round here."

Ralph piped up and asked, "Mama. Can I go with Oris to take eggs tomorrow?"

(I stopped breathing.) No way did I want that little pest going along! All he ever did was cry and get in the way and want a drink or have to go to the toilet.

"No, Ralphie, you can't go," Mom said. "Next time I take the eggs you can go with me, and I'll let you drive Sally."

Mom placed a wire basket of freshly washed eggs on the floor by the kitchen table and said, "Oris, I'm going to put the little kids to bed while you sort these eggs. Put the large ones in the brown crate and the medium-sized ones in the other crate. I want to keep the small ones to cook with."

"Dad, can I take the eggs tomorrow? That way Mom won't have to mess up her day." (Mom never had time enough to do what's needed.) "I can drive Sally, and I'll be careful and come right home."

With a smile in his dark blue eyes, Dad said, "Okay."

"Oris," Mom snapped, "for once in your life pay attention to what you're doing, and for heaven's sake, don't break any eggs."

It wasn't my fault three eggs jumped out of my hands last week and splattered all over the kitchen floor. (Mom didn't know it, but eggs are sneaky things. They look innocent, but they're not.)

Dad placed the egg-candler box on the table and lit the candle. The egg-candler consisted of a small wooden box with a hole in the top and a candle inside. When an egg was placed in front of the hole, the candle gave off enough light to see if there was a speck inside the egg. The eggs with specks, Mom saved for our use and the ones without specks were put in a large egg crate and Mom them sold to the feed store man.

"Son," Dad said. "Don't take all night candlin' them eggs 'cause that's the only candle left, and it's kinda short and won't last long."

"Okay, okay, okay, I'll hurry."

I finished candling the eggs and put the basket and egg candler away in the hall closet. I went upstairs to my room and got ready for bed.

I was excited. Sleep wouldn't come. I lay in the dark staring at the ceiling. I could see myself driving Sally to the cart, making good time because she burned up the road at a trot. I'd show Dad I was responsible. (He was always talking about me not being responsible for more than three minutes at a time.)

At breakfast, Dad said, "Hurry up and eat so ya can help me hitch the cart."

I put on a baseball cap hanging by the kitchen door and followed him out.

On the way to the barn, he said, "Sally's a bit too skittish for a little boy to handle. You drive ol' Jack. He's steady and won't give you any trouble."

I wanted to die right there on the spot! First off, I wasn't a little boy. Besides, Jack was a sway-backed, flea-bitten gray mule (at least a hundred and nine years old). He was cow-hocked. His head looked like a misshapen nail keg with the longest floppy ears nature ever put on a mule. To make matters worse, he moved slower than a fat snail on a cool fall morning.

"Dad, I'm not a little boy! When I go with Mom, she lets me drive Sally going to Cathcarts and coming home. I never have trouble with Sally."

"I know that," Dad said. "I think it's safer for you to drive ol' Jack. A bomb could go off under Jack, and he'd just switch his tail. If somethin' spooked Sally, she might take off and not stop 'til she got to Denver or San Francisco. If that happened, your mother wouldn't let me smoke in the house for six months."

Dad harnessed Jack. He laughed and said, "You hitch this fine-lookin' mule to the cart then drive on up ta the house."

A bunch of Mom's hens were busy scratching in the barnyard looking for some tasty morsel. (I aimed Jack for the hens with the intention of scattering them in a dozen directions.)

Mom came around the corner of the wood shed as ol' Jack was about to step on a hen and send the rest of them squawking and flapping their wings. "What are you doing?" She screeched.

Jack stopped, holding his right front hoof in

the air—the one he was about to set down on an unsuspecting red hen. He looked at Mom as if to say, "It ain't my fault. I didn't want to run into your prize-winning hens, but this silly little boy made me do it." (In my mind, I could see Jack was trying to make me look bad.) I drove up to the back porch.

Mom loaded a case of brown eggs and a basket full of ripe tomatoes into the cart, right at my feet. She looked me straight in the eyes and said, "Oris, you be careful, and try to do something right, just this once." (I heard ol' Jack laugh under his breath.)

With no pride left, I clucked to Jack and started down the dusty road. That darn mule wouldn't trot. He just shuffled along. Halfway to Cathcarts' we came to a dry wash. Ol' Jack stepped into the wash and stopped dead still. The basket of tomatoes slid across to the front of the cart. I leaned forward and grabbed the basket to keep it from tipping over. Right then and there, Jack raised his tail. Groaning like he was going to die, he started his process of elimination. He groaned and dumped a load of hot, smelly, green and juicy mule-apples right on my head! He wasn't satisfied with dumping on my head. That dumb mule wiggled his rump, groaned again, and deposited the rest of his green, nasty, hot, smelly mule-apples on top of the tomatoes and eggs.

After getting rid of my breakfast over the side of the cart, I dumped the eggs and tomatoes out on the ground and turned that cussed mule around and headed home. Jack was headed for the barn, so he got in a hurry for a change.

Dad met me at the barn and asked, "Why are ya back so early?" He looked at me with one eyebrow raised higher than the other. "What in the world happened to you?" I didn't answer. I jumped out of the cart and ran to the house leaving Dad to unhitch Jack.

I opened the screen door on the porch and found Mom sweeping the floor. She got this 'I- knew-something-would-go-wrong' look on her face. "Now, what have you gone and done this time?" she asked. "And what are you doing back so soon?" She glared at me. "Get out of those smelly clothes and take a bath."

"Okay," I said, and started through the kitchen door.

"Don't you dare go in the house! Take those filthy clothes off right here on the porch! I'll get the tub and put water in it while you shed those nasty things." I sat on a milk crate and removed my shoes and socks. The dried green manure-juice on my shirt and in my hair smelled worse than a dead skunk.

I knew I was in big trouble. (Mom depended on the egg money every week to help buy groceries.) Taking the eggs to Cathcarts' should've been an easy thing to do. Ol' Jack was the problem, not me. All I had to do was drive to Cathcarts, and leave the eggs and tomatoes. Then turn around and head for home.

But no! That dumb mule had to stop and drop his mule-apples on my head and the tomatoes and eggs. Mom called from the kitchen, "Pull that bench away from the wall and leave your jeans on."

"Okay," I said.

"Set the mop bucket at one end of the bench. You lie on your back with your head over the bucket so I can wash your filthy hair."

She pushed the screen door open with her right foot. In one red rubber-gloved hand, she had a milk bucket of warm water and in the other gloved hand a large pitcher of warm water. She set the bucket and pitcher down and went back in the kitchen to get soap and a towel.

"I don't know how this mess happened and I'm not sure I want to know. Your hair is full of dried, caked green manure. Hold still while I scrub your head and try to get the manure out of your hair." (She rubbed and scrubbed. I knew she'd scrubbed all my hair out by the roots.)

After two tubs of water, I still felt dirty and stinky. The rest of the day I spent hoeing weeds in the garden, and thinking all kinds of bad things about ol' Jack. Mom hollered at me once and said, "Hurry and get those weeds hoed before it snows!"

About time to start evening chores, Ralphie brought me a quart jar full of ice cold water. "Mom told me you didn't deserve it, but for me to brung you a drink anyway."

While doing my chores, I thought about ol' Jack and wished I'd never seen him.

"Hurry up, son, and finish feedin' the calves so we can go in ta supper," Dad said. "You know your mother don't like ta keep supper waitin'."

On the way to the house, Dad asked, "Ya want ta tell me what happened taday?"

"No, sir." I said.

For supper, Mom fixed fried chicken, mashed potatoes, fluffy buttermilk biscuits, corn on the cob and green beans fresh from her garden. I wasn't hungry.

All through supper, Ralphie and Eddy chattered like two magpies in a cottonwood tree. Ralphie piped up and said, "Oris, you sure did make a mess ah things, huh?"

"That's enough out of you, Ralphie," Mom said.

I helped Mom with the supper dishes. Then, I went upstairs to bed.

I lit the kerosene lamp at the head of my bed and tried to read a Captain Marvel comic book. Mom came up to tuck me in for the night. She brushed hair out of my eyes and kissed me on the forehead and said, "Sleep safe." She blew out the lamp and went back down the stairs.

A grate in the floor let heat from the kitchen into my room in the winter time. I listened at the grate to Mom and Dad talking.

They talked in low tones, but I could still hear them. Dad said, "I rode back along the road ta see if I could find what happened ta that boy and the eggs." He laughed and said, "I found eggs, tomatoes, and mule-apples in a pile. Looks like that kid threw them out after ol' Jack dumped on his head."

"It's not funny, Charles. We needed the egg money to buy groceries this week. We only have a dollar and eighty-six cents to our name."

"I know," Dad said. "We'll be okay. I won't buy cigarettes this week, and we can let the insurance premium go another week."

"Charles," Mom asked. "Is that boy going to spend the rest of his life as a disaster-looking-for-a-place-to-happen?"

I didn't wait for Dad to answer. I went back to bed and fell asleep, a tired and embarrassed little boy, not the 'man-full-grown' who had started the day.

A Perfect Understanding

"What the heck is Bert up to now?" Dad said.

Every first Saturday of the month Mom and Dad loaded us three kids into the truck, and we headed for town. Mom shopped for groceries. Dad stopped by the feed store to catch up on the latest happenings in the community.

That bright Saturday morning in May, 1944, Dad took me with him to the feed store (providing me with an escape from pushing Mom's grocery basket up and down the aisles of the Safeway store).

A half dozen ranchers and farmers, standing in the warm spring sunshine shooting the breeze, looked up the street to see what Dad was talking about. Coming down the street, hunched over on the seat of a spring wagon, sat old Bert Montague driving Toots, his ancient Mammoth Jennet. (Toots must have been at least 239 years old.) Her left ear stood straight up from her head. It appeared to be as long as I stood tall. (I was nine going on ten.) With each step, the right ear, hanging down alongside her head, swung back and forth like the pendulum of a grandfather's clock. Her head, big as a nail keg, with eyes sunk deep into a boney skull, was attached to a long skinny neck. A narrow nose sagged below her knobby knees. She was tall, sway-backed, and the color of a mouse.

Tied to the back of the wagon, a golden palomino mare mule, her ears laid flat along her neck, fought the lead rope. She pulled back and tried to brace her feet. Toots staggered but moved on.

Carl Pitkin hollered. "Bert, do ya know ya got a real live mule tied to the back of yer wagon?" Bert chose to ignore him. We watched Toots, Bert, and the agitated mule pass on down the street, around the corner, and out of sight. The rest of the rubberneckers went into the feed store office.

Dad tilted his hat to the front of his head and scratched behind his right ear. He looked down the empty street. "By cracky," he said. "That's the Dunfee mule."

Dad moved inside and took his place in the circle in front of the counter. On Saturday, the usual topics of conversation revolved around cattle, horses, mules, hogs, the price of feed, etc, but not that day. The discussion centered on the war effort and a serious mood settled over the usually joking group of weather-beaten, hard-working men. Bert and his new mule were put from their minds.

I grew uneasy. The talk of war frightened me. I

slipped out the door, stood in front of the office, and thought about Bert and his new mule.

Mom was convinced Bert owned only one pair of bib overalls, and she knew they had never seen the inside of a washing machine. Tobacco juice stained his thick, greying beard. A greasy baseball cap crowned a head of long, wild, unruly grey hair. He lived down under the hill behind the feed store on a straggly little two-acre farm surrounded on all four sides by cottonwood trees and tall brush. The small dilapidated barn and the one-room cabin reminded me of Snuffy Smith's place in the Sunday funny papers.

I crossed the empty lot behind the feed store and climbed a giant, gnarled cottonwood tree overlooking Bert's place. From there, I could see the mule tied to a post in the center of the corral. Toots stood at the watering trough treating herself to a refreshing drink. (To me, it was amazing that she could lift her big, ugly head high enough to get her nose over the edge of the trough.)

Bert came out of the barn and shuffled over to the post. He reached for the rope to untie the mule. She went crazy. She snorted and reared. With her ears laid back flat along her neck, she opened her mouth and snapped at Bert. From my perch in the old tree, I saw her mouth open wider than a crocodile's mouth in a Tarzan movie. Bert stepped back, stuffed his hands in his baggy, dirty, frayed bib overalls pockets and watched the mule trying to pull loose from the post. After a minute or two, he moseyed over to the woodpile and selected a length of firewood. He walked back to the mule and reached for the halter rope. She did a repeat performance and opened her mouth to bite his head off. A split second before her mouth snapped shut Bert shoved the wood in front of her. She got a mouthful of apple wood. She backed off. Madder than a badger in a barrel with a bulldog and with her mouth wide open, she came at him again. He gave her another mouthful of apple wood. The third time she came at him, he smacked her right between the eyes with the stick of wood. She dropped to the ground and lay like a dead cottonwood log.

Ordinarily, Bert never got in a hurry about anything. But, when that mule dropped to the ground, he moved like lightning (all 145 pounds of him), and untied the rope. He pulled her head around and sat on her neck. She tried to get up. With Bert parked on her neck, all she could do was kick, grunt, switch her tail, and raise a cloud of dust. He sat there and let her kick, grunt, and wring her tail until she wore herself out. Then he let her up. She shook her head and stood like a good mule. Bert patted her on the neck and turned her loose. I knew I had witnessed something that warm spring day which none of the neighbors would believe.

That evening I went with Grandad to feed the calves. "Grandad," I asked. "Where'd Bert come from?"

Grandad set the feed bucket on the ground and leaned against the gate. "Well, son," he said. "Nigh onta twenty year ago Bert's neighbors woke one mornin' and found 'im established in that old shack. No one knew anything 'bout 'im or where he come from, and he never volunteered no information. Ta this very day he ain't said nary a word 'bout hisself."

"Grandpa, where'd he get ol' Toots?"

"Well, son, that ugly jenny come with 'im. She was most as ugly twenty years ago as she is taday."

"She sure is ugly," I said.

Grandpa chuckled, scratched his nose and said, "There's a destiny that finds a home for ugly jennies."

After chores and supper, Mom, Dad, Grandpa, Grandma, and I sat on the porch and listened to the war news on the radio while Dad smoked his last cigarette of the day. I had been thinking about Bert and wanted to ask Dad about him. (I'd learned the hard way not to interrupt the news.) It was dark by the time the news was over. Dad's cigarette glowed red. Grandma went inside and lit the kerosene lamp in the front room. We sat on the porch in the soft glow from the lamp.

"Dad," I asked. "How old is Bert?"

"I don't know, son. Don't know much about him. I do know he's a very private person, a hard worker and he keeps busy."

"That he does," Grandad said. "He trades for

donkeys, goats, chickens, rabbits, mules, and does anything else he can do ta make a dime."

"There is a hint of the old south in that gentle drawl of his. I tell you, there is more to Bert than meets the eye," Grandma said.

Mom wasn't fond of Bert. She said, "He needs to wash his shirt and overalls, take a bath and comb his hair. And, besides that, he has a personality like Attila the Hun."

Dad said, "I'm sure the mule Bert and Toots were dragging down the street is the Dunfee mule."

I asked him, "Who's the Dunfee mule?"

Grandad answered. "In the '20's and the early '30's, Ray Dunfee lived over ta the east of us on the old Morgan place. He hadda small herd of top-quality mares. Some of 'em had some Tennessee Walker blood. One of his better mares produced a filly that was a cut above the rest. Ray named 'er Abby."

Dad said, "Three years later, your grandad and I were helpin' the Dunfees build a new barn. We were there the morning Abby came in with a palomino mule foal at her side."

Grandad laughed so hard he could hardly talk and then said, "Ray Dunfee couldn't believe his eyes. Right there on the spot exactly, a whole new vocabulary of colorful words was invented."

Dad continued, "Mr. Dunfee hated mules more than he hated cat manure. When the mule was a yearling, he sold her to Cap Wilson. Cap kept her until she was a three-year old. He couldn't do a thing with her so she went through the auction. She ended up in a rodeo bucking string. That mule Toots dragged down the street today has gotta be that Dunfee mule."

From then on, when we went to town, every chance I got, I'd 'lite out' for the cottonwood tree. At times, I thought the mule would stomp Bert into the ground. Slowly but surely, she calmed down. By late summer, Bert tied the mule to one of Toots' hames, and she went everywhere Bert went. He plowed and cultivated gardens and hauled trash. Folks got used to seeing the three of them going about their business. By this time, Dad was sure she was the Dunfee mule.

Bert worked with the mule all winter long. Spring arrived with a flourish. Folks thought Bert would sell his mule or trade her off. Summer came. When asked what he was going to do with the mule, Bert's reply was always the same—"I'll feed her."

One afternoon, Bert caught me in the tree and motioned for me to come down. I climbed out of the tree and crossed through the hedge. Bert, standing in the barn door chewing on a straw, looked at me and asked, "Does your pop pay you tah spy on honest folks?"

"No sir," I said. "He doesn't know I'm here."

"You Charlie's boy, Oris. Right?"

Before I could answer, he continued. "If you'll keep

this mule a secret, I'll let you help when you come to town."

Fall passed and winter came again. Bert worked with his mule several hours a day. On Saturdays, I begged Mom to let me go to town with her and Dad so I could visit Bert. She didn't think I should spend so much time with Bert. She'd say, "He doesn't bathe, shave or change clothes and isn't the right example for a growing boy."

"Aah, Mom," I'd whine. And she'd let me go.

Bert was fun to be around, and he treated me like a man-full-grown.

Under Bert's gentle hand and talented training, the mule became a willing, gentle creature. When I rode her, Bert no longer kept a rope on her. I rode her all over his little place. March presented a mild and pleasant month for a change, perfect weather for training a mule. I arrived at Bert's one Saturday morning to find Stella (that's what Bert called her) tied in front of the barn sporting an English saddle. "Well kid, today we start getting serious with this little girl."

The arrival of spring gave new life to all God's creatures, even Bert. He smiled a lot—even whistled some of the time. To this day, I don't know if Bert trained Stella or Stella influenced Bert.

Mom came home from town late one Tuesday and said, "Bert must be sick. I met the rascal on the street and he said 'hello' and tipped his hat."

Dad's blue eyes smiled and he asked Mom, "Have you had a sunstroke?"

Spring work was in full swing at home. It was the middle of May before I saw Bert and Stella again. Bert still needed to comb his hair, his overalls would still stand alone when he took them off at night, he was happy and smiling. Stella was as gentle as a little girl's calico kitten.

One bright Saturday morning, Bert saddled Stella. While I sat on the top rail of the corral he made two trips around the field at a walk. He rode up to the corral and said, "Watch this." Stella moved out in a gait which was called a 'Fox Trot'. Twice around the field, Stella performed perfectly. As young as I was, I realized a perfect understanding existed between the man and the mule. Bert (I would later learn) rode in perfect dressage form.

The cottonwood leaves whispered their secrets around the little farm.

I was sitting on the top rail of the corral. Bert rode up and started telling me about his life before he came to our county. He was born and raised on a horse-breeding farm in Warren, Tennessee. He was forty years old when his father died. He had a falling out with his sister over the estate, left Tennessee, and never returned. A lonely, bitter man, his life turned for the better on the day he took a donkey to the auction. He found a seat on the top row in the sale barn and settled in to watch and see how much his donkey would bring.

Bert said, "A group of five horses and one palomino mule slated for the killers trotted into the ring. I watched as they trotted by, the mule going at a slight gait. After a few minutes, I was convinced she was gaited. My bid was $35, and I came away owning an outlaw mule."

Bert chuckled and continued, "It took five men tah get a halter on that mule. I drove Toots and the wagon into the pen, and it took all five men tah get her tied to the wagon. She was a mule with a 'definite opinion'. She fought all the way home, and Toots was worn to a frazzle.

"Kid," he said. "I'm taking Stella to the county fair this fall."

'Yeah right,' I thought.

"Sounds good," I said. "I promise I won't tell a living soul about Stella or what you've told me."

Bert and Toots didn't do much garden work that summer. Bert spent most of everyday working with Stella.

The first of September rolled around. Fall was thick in the air. The fair opened on September 3rd. Saturday was the big day—it was Rodeo Day. Farm and ranch folk put work aside. Stores in town closed. The grandstand filled with smiling, laughing, happy people. The high school band struck up the National Anthem. The crowd in the grandstand stood. Men and boys removed their hats, and hands were placed over hearts. The outgoing rodeo queen, Mary Alice Carter, astride a glistening black horse, carried the flag. She entered the arena at a canter and circled, followed by a small army of men, women and kids riding their horses. Twice around the arena they rode and then exited.

The crowd, in a festive mood, cheered bronc riders, bull riders, ropers, barrel racers, chuck wagon races, harness races, and horse races. Old records were broken, new records set to the sound of honking horns, whistling, cheering and firecrackers. The clown was the hit of the day. People from miles around had trucked their saddle horses and ponies to the fairgrounds to be a part of the mass ride after the final event.

The new rodeo queen, Joylyn Webster, carrying the stars and stripes rode into the arena. The crowd went wild—cheering, whistling, and stomping their feet. She was followed by a wave of horsemen who lined up two-deep and faced the grandstand. The flag unfurled to begin the final pass.

The crowd fell silent as a golden palomino mule entered the arena at a Fox Trot. Her rider, a man in a black derby hat, black swallow-tailed coat, and shiny black riding boots, rode in perfect form—a sight never before seen in this community. Mule and rider took their place at the end of the line. The mule stood perfectly still, with her long, slender ears pointed straight ahead, chin tucked under, and an arch in her neck.

The flag started its pass in front of the massed riders. The riders removed their hats. A murmur rippled through the grandstand when the Mystery Man on the golden palomino mule removed his derby and the crowd recognized the eccentric Bert. The riders followed the flag out of the arena. Bert and his mule brought up the end of the procession.

The loudspeaker crackled and popped. The announcer said, "Will the gentleman on the mule please come to the stand?" Bert turned the mule and rode at a canter to the stand. The announcer leaned over the rail and talked with Bert for a few minutes.

The crowd was silent.

The loudspeaker crackled and the announcer said, "Our own Albert Montague, formerly of Warren, Tennessee, has agreed to give us a demonstration ride on Stella, his gaited mule."

Bert rode to the front of the grandstand, tipped his derby to the crowd, and Stella bowed. Turning Stella to the left, they moved out at a Fox Trot. The crowd was silent. Halfway around the arena, Stella changed to another gait. The crowd went wild! Whistling and shouting, the spectators poured out of the bleachers like a giant wave and surrounded Bert and Stella. Hands were extended to Bert.

A new Bert, and Stella, no longer the Dunfee mule, exited the arena that day in 1945.

Ol' Blue and Charlie

"Oris, for once in your life, will you sit down to eat your breakfast? For heaven's sake, chew your food and drink your milk." Mom was winding up for a nagging speech. (I couldn't wait to get out of the house before she got started.) "Furthermore, you have no business going up on the mountain by yourself today – or any day, so far as that goes."

"But M-a-a-w-m, Dad said I could go."

"I don't care what your Dad said. You have no business up there alone."

What did she know about anything, anyway? I had my donkey, ol' Blue, and Ring, my long-haired black dog, going with me. I was eleven years old and didn't need anyone telling me what I could or couldn't do.

"Where on that mountain are you going?" She asked. "Every time I ask you a question, you say you don't know. Well, young man, you tell me where you're going and when you'll be back, or by thunder, you won't go! Do you hear me?"

Past experience had taught me when she said, "Do

73

you hear me?" I'd better turn on the innocent look I had developed into an art for just such occasions, and give her the answer she wanted.

"I'm going up the old clay road to the west side of the rockslide." Wearing my much practiced 'innocent look' that usually got me out of trouble, I looked her straight in the eye and said, "Gee, Mom, I'm sorry about last Saturday. I won't let it happen again."

At the time, I didn't think much about it. Now, that I am older and wiser (my wife, Pat, will debate my being 'wiser'), I often think about what could have happened that September day in 1945. It's a wonder, in my youthful ignorance, ol' Blue and I didn't do more harm than good.

That September morning started like any other Saturday morning. I was out of bed by 5:00 a.m. Mom snapped from her bedroom, "Quit clattering around and let the rest of us sleep."

Living on a ranch meant extra chores each Saturday. This morning, I was going up on the mountain to gather pine cones. Mr. Kissinger, the owner of the local hardware store, paid me two cents a dozen for all the big pine cones I could bring to his store.

Ol' Blue, Ring and I had spent the last three weekends up on the mountain gathering cones. Last Saturday, Ring had run two different rabbits into their holes at two different times. I wondered if that crazy dog knew he'd never catch a rabbit. The first rabbit scampered into the safety of its hole behind a Yucca plant. Ring looked at me with a look that said, "Ain't you gonna get outta that cart and help me dig this here rabbit outta it's hole?" Naturally, an effort had to be made to help Ring flush the rabbit. Pine-cone picking came to a halt. Ring wouldn't give up. He was sure he could dig a rabbit out of its hole. The crazy dog didn't know the rabbit had a back door he used to escape from pesky dogs. It was the rabbit's fault we were late getting to the pine cones. (Sometimes rabbits will interfere to keep young boys from executing their well-laid plans.)

Time slipped away and darkness came creeping down the side of the mountain before the cart was filled with cones. It was deep-down 'coal dark' by the time we descended onto the county road. In my mind, I saw all kinds of scary evil shapes floating across the road in front of us as ol' Blue pulled the cart over the road toward home. She never flicked an ear. I wasn't that brave. Today, I wanted to get an early start so I could be home before dark.

Chores were finished in record time and breakfast downed in a few gulps. I fed, curried, brushed, harnessed and hooked ol' Blue to the cart before she knew what had happened. At last, we were on our way.

"Don't be in such a ram-roddin' rush," Mom called as we drove past the porch. She handed me a jug of water and a Karo syrup bucket containing lunch.

"Mind you don't drink out of the creek. There's no telling what germs are swimming around in that water. Young man, you make sure you're home by chore time. You hear me?"

Brutus, Mom's big Rhode Island Red rooster, crowed as we drove past the chicken coop. He was saying, "I hope you're late gettin' home and get in big trouble." (Roosters like to see young boys get in trouble.)

"Thanks for the lunch, Mom. You make the best lunches." I figured it wouldn't cause me pain to elaborate on the lunch. (Moms like to hear those kinda things.) "Don't worry. I'll be home in time to do chores."

When we reached the county road, Ring jumped into the cart and sat on the seat beside me. The cooing of a mourning dove broke the early morning silence. The trace chains on the harness jingled a cheerful tune as we made our way along the road. What else did I need? I owned the best donkey in the county. My faithful dog was by my side. I planned to make a small fortune gathering cones. Best of all, I managed to keep Mom from thinking I should take my bothersome little brother with me. I felt like a man-full-grown.

The county road ended about two miles from our house. From the end of the road, we followed a trail to the creek. When we got to the creek, ol' Blue didn't want to get her feet wet. She was determined that no amount of urging would coax her into the water. Slapping her rump with the lines didn't work. Using my Scout knife, I cut a switch off a tree (with which an effort was made to encourage her). Still, she refused to budge. Trying to lead her into the water failed. The harder I pulled on the bit ring, the longer her neck stretched (at least to a length of five or six feet).

Ring stood with his head cocked first one way then another, taking in the whole scene. Suddenly, he started barking and nipping at ol' Blue's heels. Across the creek she bolted, knocking me off balance and into the water. When Blue, the cart, and the dog reached the other side, Blue stopped and turned to look at me as if to say, "What's wrong with you? I'm gonna tell the whole world how stupid you looked lying on your back in the crick."

Sixty-five years later, I can still see that blue donkey hooked to the cart, looking at me with the corners of her mouth turned up and a twinkle in her eye. By the time I waded across the creek, I was laughing, too.

The rest of the way up the mountain was uneventful. The warm sun dried my wet clothes, ol' Blue was making good time. A piñon squawker (blue jay) scolded us as we rattled past his tree. He said, "What is you and that funny-lookin' donkey doin' trespassin' on my mountain?" (Ring was off chasing a rabbit and was spared the Squawker's agitated chatter.) About an hour later, we reached the cone-picking area.

I looped the lines around the left hame on the collar. Ol' Blue, like the good donkey she was, stood patiently while I filled a bucket with shiny cones and emptied them into the cart. She followed as I moved further into the trees.

When I first arrived, I noticed a black saddled horse standing in an open area. I looked around several times, but didn't see anyone. Ring started barking at something in a thicket of currant bushes. Ol' Blue began to get nervous. She stood with her ears alert and pointed toward the thicket. Ring ventured into the bushes. I could hear someone talking to him. "Good dog. Easy, boy. Where'd you come from?"

I set my half-filled bucket down and cautiously walked over to the bushes. I discovered a man lying on his back on the ground. He looked up at me and said, "Damn, kid. Am I ever glad to see you. My horse bucked me off and I'm in one hell-uva-fix."

Ring walked up to him and gave him a warm, wet lick in the left ear.

I responded by saying, "You don't look like much of a cowboy to me." As soon as the words dropped out of my mouth, I was sorry I'd said anything. (All at once, I didn't feel very smart.) I could tell at a glance he was in bad shape. His right leg was twisted and lying at an awkward angle. A trickle of blood showed at the left corner of his mouth. I felt as dumb as the knots on a potato. I knew he needed help.

"Mister." I said. "I'll go get some help." In one frantic sweep, I gathered the lines from the hame on ol' Blue's collar and jumped in the cart.

"Hey, Kid! Wait a minute. Kid, how big is that cart?"

"Big enough to hold two bales of hay." I said.

"Can you back that cart close and help me into it so you can get me outta here? I need to get to a doctor as soon as possible."

Ol' Blue did her part and backed the cart into the thicket. (The look on her face told me she had been saving lives for a long time.)

"Kid," he said. "We'll need some sticks and something to bind them in place so we can make a splint."

Out came my Scout knife. I cut three large currant stalks. Next, I caught his horse and removed one of the bridle reins. We made a splint for his injured leg. By the time we finished the splint, I was scared. I was nervous. I was shaking like an aspen leaf in the wind. To make matters worse, when he tried to move, it appeared he might have a broken rib or two.

"Take your belt and fasten it to mine. We'll cinch it around my chest," he said. "We'll see if that helps."

When I tightened the belts around his chest, he let loose with a string of cuss words I had never heard in all the years of my sheltered life. He cussed with feeling and eloquence. (Later, when I grew old enough to cuss, I tried to cuss with the eloquence he used that day on the mountain.) Through it all, ol' Blue stood as still as thick cream in a jar.

Getting him into the cart was no easy task. I spread my coat on top of the cones. (No way would I take the cones out.) The cart box was short. His good leg hung over the end gate. Ol' Blue willingly gave up her collar pad for a cushion to protect his leg from the tailgate.

No room remained in the cart for me. I jumped on ol' Blue's back and we started down the mountain. The Miller place was the closest. We headed there. Every time the cart hit a bump and jolted, the injured man yelled or cussed, sometimes both.

Would ol' Blue cross the crick? Upon reaching the water's edge, she stopped dead-in-her-donkey-tracks and lowered her head to sniff the water. She raised her head and told me if I forced her into the crick, she would tell my mother I wanted to wear a white starched shirt to sunday school. (Sometimes donkeys will resort to such dirty tricks.) I kicked her in the ribs and slapped her rump with the doubled-up lines. Ring got into the act again. A few nips at ol' Blue's heels and she stepped into the water. Halfway across, she stopped and tried to lie down. The shafts on the cart kept her from lying down all the way, but she kept trying. During ol' Blue's shenanigans, I got my second dunking of the day. (If I'd had a gun, I woulda shot that donkey graveyard-dead right there in the middle of the crick.) The cussin' and hollerin' from the cart led me to believe my injured passenger felt the same way.

By the time I opened the gate into Miller's horse pasture, Ring was barking at their front door. Years later, Mrs. Miller told me she would always remember that day and the sight of a wet boy on a wet blue roan donkey pulling a cart. Tied to the cart was a black horse and hanging out the end of the cart was a man's leg.

The Millers placed a mattress in the bed of their pickup and helped the visibly shaken man from the cart and onto the mattress. The mattress would make his ride to the hospital a little more comfortable than his trip off the mountain.

Mrs. Miller pinched my left cheek and said, "You're a good little boy."

I'd had enough of the injured man, and didn't want Mrs. Miller pinching my cheek again and calling me 'a good little boy'. I climbed into the cart, whistled for Ring, and went back up the mountain to pick more pine cones.

Late one afternoon several weeks later while I was feeding the chickens, a pickup drove into the yard. Ring barked like he'd never seen a pickup before. (I think he barked sometimes just to hear his head rattle.) I ambled over to the chicken-yard fence and watched a man on crutches get out of the passenger's side. Mom came from the house to meet him. He said something to her. She pointed to me.

"Oris, come here," Mom called.

I turned and started toward the gate. Standing between me and the gate was Brutus, Mom's red rooster, with his feathers ruffled and strutting back and forth. He looked at me and said, "What ya doin'? I've a good mind to peck your eyes out. Try to get past me and you'll wish ya'd never been born." He threw his cigar away, spread his wings and came at me. I tossed a handful of corn at him. (The greedy bird forgot all about me.)

"Do you know this man?" Mom asked.

I answered, "No, Ma'am."

"I'm Charlie Vicman," he said, "the not-so-very-good cowboy you hauled off the mountain." Then he laughed.

Mom gave me her silent "What-have-you-been-up-to?" look.

Charlie handed me a package wrapped in brown paper and tied with white string. "This is for you," he said.

I took the package and stood looking at the ground. (Sometimes young boys are quiet even though mothers can't remember a time when they were.)

Charlie put his arm around my shoulders and said, "Go ahead and open it."

I broke the string and opened the package. Inside was a blue western shirt. I knew I should say something (but my brain ran away and my mouth wouldn't work).

I stood and brushed at my jeans with my right hand.

"Tell the man 'thank you'," Mom said.

I looked at Charlie. (The smile on his face went all the way around to the back of his neck.) "Thank you, sir, for the shirt."

"What's this all about?" Mom asked.

Charlie sat down on the porch steps and proceeded to tell how his horse had thrown him onto a large rock and broke his leg. Then I came along and hauled him off the mountain in my cart. As he talked to Mom and filled her in on the details, I began to think Charlie was okay.

"Mr. Vicman, Oris has a habit of not telling us what he does or what goes on in his own private little world. He hadn't breathed a word about you." Then she invited him to supper to meet Dad. I was okay with that.

That fall and winter Charlie spent a lot of time at our house. He and my parents became close friends. As time went on, from him, I learned to appreciate good books. He made *Les Miserables* come alive for me. To this day, *A Tale of Two Cities* is one of my favorites.

Charlie wouldn't have joined a club. He wasn't much for going to church. He cussed some, maybe even bent the law a little, and he liked a shot of whiskey once in a while, but he was my idol.

The following 4th of July will forever be a special

day in my life. Charlie won the Bareback Bronc ride at the rodeo.

I was proud to be his friend.

A Man Full-Grown and His Donkey

Supper was almost over. Dad savored the last bite of blueberry cobbler and laid his fork on the plate. He looked at me and said, "Son. There's a stray donkey in the pasture with yer donkey, Blue. First thing in the mornin' after breakfast, you'd best go run that donkey out on the county road. He'll find his way home, wherever that is."

I panicked! I took a deep breath and swallowed a couple of times. My hands started to sweat. My heart tried to jump out of my chest. My voice squeaked as I said, "I bought him from Bert."

I held my breath and waited for Dad's reply. He took his time shaking out his napkin and slowly dabbed the left corner of his mouth. By now, I had to breathe, but was afraid to let my breath out because it would rush like a great blast of wind. Mom stopped eating. (The look on her brow indicated a severe storm was about to hit. She, along with my two small brothers, waited for Dad to explode.)

"Now let me git this straight," Dad said. "Ya bought

that donkey from ol' Bert without askin' me first. First off, you shoulda asked me. Secondly, what in Sam Hill did ya use fer money?"

"Bert only wanted ten dollars for the donkey. I had five dollars in quarters."

"Oris, five dollars in quarters don't make ten dollars."

"I know. I traded five of my 4-H hens for the rest—the donkey's name is Jim."

"You did what? Have you lost your mind?" Mom hit the table with her right fist, rattling every dish. She screeched, "For one thing, we don't need another donkey on this place! Those hens were your 4-H projects. Money's tight around here right now. We need all the eggs we can sell. What in the world were you thinking? As usual, you were NOT thinking!"

She looked at Dad and sighed, "I'm at my wits' end with this kid."

For once, my two younger brothers were quiet. Being quiet didn't keep them from looking all smirky. I was in trouble. They were enjoying every second of it.

"Son," Dad said, "Bert did some tradin' with Mel Anderson. That's how he happened ta have the donkey. That donkey bluffed out the Anderson kids. They can't ride him. They can't drive him. He kicks and bites and is all around a badly spoiled donkey."

I sat in my chair trying to think of something to say. My thinker failed me. My mouth was dry. My heart dropped clear to my toes. I knew I was dead. Dad finished what he had to say and waited for me to answer. I looked to Mom, hoping she'd come to my rescue.

"You got yourself in this mess, now get yourself out of it," she said, her voice dripping icicles.

The palms of my hands sweat like they did in Sunday School when Miss Perkins asked for volunteers to read a verse from the Bible. What was I to do? I wanted desperately to keep Jim. I knew I had to come up with an iron-clad reason and quick. Like the neon sign flashing in the window of Al's Barber Shop, an idea began to burn in my fuzzy brain.

"Dad. I've always wanted another donkey to drive with ol' Blue."

"Son, I just told ya, the Anderson kids couldn't do a thing with that donkey. What makes ya think you can?"

"I know I should've asked you first before I bought him. Everyone says you're the best hand with a mule in the whole county, and I knew you'd help me straighten him out. Then I'd have the best team of donkeys around." My heart was no longer beating. (The only reason I was still alive was my body didn't know my heart had stopped.) It was news to me that Jim had so many bad habits.

Dad glanced at Mom, then across the table at my brothers. They were smiling from ear-to-ear like two impish elves, enjoying every second of my uneasiness. Dad looked me square in the eye. "Tomorrow mornin' ya bring them donkeys home. After I set the water on the hay, that Anderson donkey and me'll have ta educate ya."

"Thanks, Dad. I'll have 'em home early." I breathed a sigh of relief. My heart started beating again. I began to think I'd live.

Dad leaned back in his chair. From his left shirt pocket, he pulled a Bull Durham tobacco sack and rolled a cigarette. I thought I saw a hint of a twinkle in his eye when he looked across the table at Mom. He scratched a match on the bottom of his chair. I watched as he lit the cigarette. All trace of what might have been a twinkle in his eye had vanished. (Not breathing regularly, I was now seeing things that weren't there.) It must have been my imagination. Dad pushed his squeaky old chair back from the table, got up, and went out on the back steps to enjoy his last smoke of the day. When the screen door shut, I started breathing again.

Ralphie, my smart-alecky middle brother said, "Boy, I thought you was really gonna catch it from Dad, and I'll bet you can't do a thing with that dumb donkey. I hope you have to sell him and Blue both."

Not to be out done by his partner in crime, my little brother, Eddie, asked Mom, "Why didn't Daddy get mad at Oris for buyin' another donkey? 'Specially without askin' first."

"That's enough, you two. It's not your affair. Put your dirty plates in the sink and be off with you."

I started to clear my dishes from the table. Mom motioned for me to sit in a chair.

"Why didn't you ask your father before going off half-cocked and buying that donkey?"

"I don't know. I guess I wasn't thinking."

"Well, if you don't know, who does? Young man, you'd better start thinking. Do you hear me?"

Dad hadn't told me to take Jim back. He was going to help me with him. Now, Mom got into the act. When she used that tone of voice, experience had taught me she was gearing up for a long lecture. No way did I want to face her or her practical way of thinking. For once in their lives, my two pesky brothers arrived when needed. Entering the kitchen, Ralphie said, "Mama, can we ride our bikes for a while?"

Mom looked at the kitchen clock and said, "No. It's time you got ready for bed." I knew she'd have her hands full for a few minutes. I took advantage of the situation and slipped out the kitchen door.

Dad, sitting on the porch steps finishing his cigarette, said, "Son, will ya shut the chicken house door? If we leave the door open and a skunk raids the chicken house, your Mom'll have my head and yours, too. When that's done, come back, and we'll have a talk."

A knot grew in the pit of my stomach. My imagination kicked into high gear. Had he changed his mind? Was he going to tell me Jim had to go?

I shut the chicken house door. My stomach was plain sick with worry. I plopped down by Dad and watched him take the last drag on what seemed to be the end of his fingers. He always got his money's worth out of a cigarette. He carefully set the very small cigarette butt on the step. With the heel of his badly scuffed left black boot, he ground it into a small spot of light grey ashes.

With a very dry mouth, and a knot in the pit of my stomach, I waited for him to say something. He wasn't one for rushing into anything. I wanted to get this talk behind me.

"Son. Any boy fit to own a donkey can ride, drive, and work his donkey. If he can't, he'd best get rid o' the critter and get hisself a lamb." He added insult to injury by saying, "No boy worth his salt would let a donkey get the best o' him, no matter how ornery the donkey or how many boys he had buffaloed. Are you man enough ta tackle that donkey in the mornin'?"

"Yes, sir," I answered.

Come morning, I was up and had most of my chores done before Dad came to the barn. I milked two cows to his one. (He wasn't keen on milking anyway.) Dad fed the cows and calves. I swept the barn floor and fed the pigs and was ready to go to breakfast. But 'no-o-o'. Dad had to stop and check Mom's garden. (As if it wouldn't be there after breakfast.)

Halfway through breakfast, Ralphie piped up, "Daddy are you gonna make Oris take that donkey back?" I wanted to punch him a good one. However, from experience, I knew hitting my brother wasn't the thing to do, especially at the table. The look on my face told the little twerp he was in for it the first time I caught him out of Mom's sight.

After breakfast, Dad shouldered his shovel and walked up the ditch to change the water. Hot-footing it over to the pasture, I caught Blue and tied her to the fence. With halter in hand, I walked up to Jim. He stood still as honey in a glass jar. He put his nose into the noseband, and I fastened the halter. 'Heck fire, no trouble here,' I thought. 'This donkey's gonna be okay.'

Blue was a good traveler. She walked fast for a donkey and Jim kept pace with her. All the way home, he didn't let the lead rope tighten. He let me catch him without any problem, and he led better than most horses. I was beginning to think that maybe Mr. Anderson was wrong about him.

As we turned into the driveway, one of my brothers threw a handful of gravel at Jim's feet. Blue shied away from the gravel intended for Jim. The gravel didn't bother him. Dad was still setting the water on the hay, so I turned Blue and Jim loose in the corral.

Over an hour passed. Dad still hadn't come to the

house. Patience not being one of my virtues, I went back to the corral to issue to Jim his proper call as a beast of burden. With bridle in hand, I put my arm around his neck. He stood as calm and peaceful as apple pie on Sunday. I tried to put the bit in his mouth. He didn't want any part of that foolishness. He clamped his teeth together like a four-inch vise. No amount of prying or forcing succeeded in getting the bit into his mouth. All at once he turned into a hurricane of hair, mouth, long ears and feet that twisted-turned-jumped and bucked, trying to dislodge me and the hated bridle.

He stopped, turned in a tight circle and whopped me in the chest with his head. The breath blew out of me. I lay on my back in the dust and looked up to see him coming at me with all the furor of an Arkansas tornado – his mouth wide open, lips drawn back, his ears laid back along his neck, and his eyes sparking fire. I rolled under the bottom pole of the corral as he came to a sliding, dusty halt. He stared at me through the poles of the corral with the most 'un-adult-er-ated' hatred I'd ever seen in any eye.

I was so mad I could 'spit' (and I did). I stood up, dusted off my shirt and Levis and crawled through the rails back into the corral. That durn donkey stood on the far side of the corral, head lowered, looking at some imaginary mouthful of grass. I approached him with caution. He raised his head. Faking innocence, he looked at me with big brown eyes as if to say, "Well, little boy, how are you this fine day?"

Jim surprised me. He lowered his head and took the bit like it was no big deal. The next step was to harness him. He followed like a lamb as I led him to the barn and tied him to the hitch ring by the door. I came out of the door with a harness over my right shoulder. He turned his rump to me and started kicking like all get-out. It was plain to see he didn't want any part of that harness. To make matters worse, trying to get away from that durn kicking donkey, I tripped over my own feet ending up on the dusty ground tangled in the harness. Hearing a chuckle, I looked up from my undignified position to see Dad sitting on the top pole of the corral (and to see that durn donkey grinning from ear-to-ear).

"Well, boy, are ya gonna put the harness on that donkey or hav' ya decide ta wear it yerself?" he asked.

That did it! Upon removing myself from the tangle of straps, I brushed the dust off my shirt, walked over to Jim, and kicked him a good one right in the ribs. He kicked at me! I kicked him again. He kicked at me. I kicked him. His next kick caught me right in the gut, sending me rolling into a corral post.

"Don't let that donkey git the best of ya," Dad said. "Keep away from his hind feet! Could be he don't like the way you comb yer hair or somethin'." These were words that drifted down to me as I lay in the dust gasping for air. In my awkward position, I didn't appreciate the advice Dad was offering. My legs were shaking. I stood up and brushed the dust from my shirt and leaned against the post to catch my breath.

"Are ya OK?" Dad asked from his perch.

Of course, I was OK! After three more tries, Jim stopped bucking and kicking and let me put the harness on him. By then, I was one worn out thirteen-year-old boy.

Dad said, "Leave the harness on that rascal and tie him ta the hitch ring. That way he can contemplate the events o' the mornin' while we go up ta the house for a cold drink o' water. It sure did make me tired and thirsty watchin' you and that donkey jiggin' around."

Everyday for three days, Jim and I battled it out. No way did he want to be a self-respecting donkey and wear a harness. He didn't like the bit. He didn't like the collar. He darn sure didn't like the harness.

Late Saturday afternoon, Dad stopped to check and see how things were going. He said, "Are ya spendin' most o' the time lyin' in the dust? Yer mother tells me every time she looks out the kitchen window you're lyin' on the ground or brushin' dust off yer shirt and jeans."

One Friday morning, with bridle in hand, I approached Jim prepared to do battle. Something was wrong. He didn't fight the bridle and stood calm as peaches and cream while I tied him to the hitch ring. With caution, I placed the harness on his back. No trouble here. He stood calm and quiet. At last, my persistence had paid off. I felt like a man full-grown. I'd stayed with it and hadn't let that blue roan donkey bluff me like he had the Anderson kids. I patted him on the neck. I thought, 'You ol' rascal. You ain't as tuff as you thought you were.'

Wanting to show off a little, I went looking for Dad. He was in the shop putting new sections in the mower knife. "Dad, that durn donkey isn't so tuff after all. He's standing at the hitch ring harnessed and ready to be hooked to the cart." Dad laid the ball peen hammer on the work bench. As he turned to face me, I thought I saw the trace of a smile on his face. (It must have been my imagination.)

"Let's go have a look at 'im, " Dad said.

"Jim took the bit and stood still while I harnessed him. He finally decided he couldn't get the best of me." I said.

Dad stood by the gate and looked at Jim. "From the way he's standin' there, hip-shot, ears droopin', and eyes half shut, he don't seem much worried 'bout a thing," Dad mumbled. "Well, son, you gonna stand there all day and admire that donkey instead o' hitchin' him ta that cart Should we take the harness off him and go fishin'?"

"Let's go fishin'," I said.

No argument there. I liked to fish as well as any boy in two counties. I'd been wanting to go fishing ever since school let out for the summer. However, Dad always found something that needed to be done. Every time I asked him if I could go fishing, he'd always say, "When we git work caught up."

"Reckon we could ride them donkeys over ta the fishin' hole?" Dad asked. He smiled and said, "You git Blue and I'll git them poles. Days like this are made fer breathin' God's fresh air and fishin'."

Grandad, with a shovel over his shoulder, stopped to see how things were going with Jim and me. "Seems like you and that donkey are no longer havin' a permanent disagreement over what is expected of 'im. Gittin' that donkey ta do what ya wanted 'im ta do seemed to be as hard as sneakin' a sunrise past a rooster," Grandad said. "But remember this, patience is the price of survival."

Son. Will it be okay with you if I ride Jim and you ride Blue?" Dad asked.

"Fine with me."

Dad went to the shop to get the fishing poles. I grabbed a shovel and headed for the garden to dig some worms.

By the time I got back to the barn with the worms, Dad had bridled Blue and Jim. "That donkey couldn't 'ave behaved any better," he said. "He took the bit like it was the thing ta do, no fuss at all."

After inspecting the worms and commenting on how any self-respecting fish couldn't possibly pass up such a tasty morsel, he handed me my fishing pole and told me to go ahead on and open the gate.

I felt like giving Jim a whack with my pole. After all the trouble I'd been having with him, with Dad, he behaved as calm as Mom's pet yellow cat. I was beginning to think that dumb donkey was just trying to make me look bad.

Aggravated as I was with Jim, I laughed when Dad came riding through the gate. I'd never seen him on a donkey. There he was, brown Stetson hat set firm and proper, long legs which took the soles of his scuffed black boots to within inches of the ground, holding a fishing pole in one hand, and guiding Jim with the other.

"Whatcha laughin' at?" he quipped, as he rode through the gate with the exaggerated air of someone of great importance. "Leave the gate open. Yer Mom'll be home soon. She won't have ta git out of the car ta open the gate. Nothin' makes a woman madder than having ta open a gate, 'specially, if the menfolks have gone fishin'. I don't know what it is women have against fishin'."

"Hey, Men!" Grandad hailed. "How come I have ta tend this water while you two goof off?"

"Because we're better lookin'." Dad hollered back.

Grandad walked over to the fence. "Well, boy, how goes the donkey business?"

Okay. I said. "We're goin' fishin'."

"I'm glad ya told me," he said. "Otherwise, I'd o' thought you was just takin' them fishin' poles fer a ride."

Dad and Grandad discussed the hot weather, how it seemed early for it to be so hot and dry. They hoped there would be enough irrigation water for the rest of the summer. Grandad told us he and Elmer reached an agreement just a little while ago on who would use the water and when. If Elmer so much as tampered with the head gate while Grandad was using the water, he'd find his hair parted with Grandad's #2 irrigating shovel. Dad thought that should be easy enough for Elmer to understand.

On arriving at the creek, Dad said, "Make sure Jim's tied to where he can't git loose. I darn sure don't wanna walk home havin' ta carry all them fish we'll catch." Past experience had proven to me he would catch the most fish, and I'd end up carrying them.

Dad had his special way of fishing. It was a ritual that had been handed down to him from his father. First thing, he would check to see at which angle the shadows of the trees were falling. Then, he would find a 'magic' spot on the bank to set the can of worms. Many times he had instructed me in the art of placing the worm can. If the can were too close to the bank, the fish would jump out of the water to get at the worms. (Of course, there would be no sport in that.) Next, he positioned his hat on the back of his head. It took several tries before the hat was just right. (Heaven forbid if the brim should shade his face!) Trout could see his eyes in the shade of his hat brim and then escape to the deep, black recesses of the fishin' hole. He'd sit on the ground 'just the right distance' from the can of worms and roll a cigarette. The last, and final part of the time-honored ritual before putting the worm on the hook, was to place the freshly rolled cigarette in the left corner of his mouth. Holding the fish hook exactly six inches from his mouth, he'd spit on the hook and light the cigarette. All this preparation would be to no avail if the fat, red worm wasn't placed on the hook head end first.

The long hot summer afternoon stretched out before us – a time of lazy, effortless fishing.

For the rest of my life, I would remember that gentle afternoon in the summer of 1946.

When Dad started to talk, even the rocks and trees stopped to listen. He referred to times like this as quality time. He talked to me about always being honest in everything I did during my life—look for an honest cause to champion and give it my best – let people know where I stand on every issue, be it good or bad—always be respectful and kind to older people and those younger than me (even my two brothers)— for an honest dollar, do an honest day's work – believe in God and Country—realize every man can't be a poet no more'n a sheep can be a donkey—always remember the only thing gossip can't hurt is live sheep or dead people—pay attention to my own business—take care of my own problems—remember, all people, no matter the color of their skin or their station in life, are the same under the skin in every important way. They desire to eat, to sleep, to be dry and warm and safe against the coming day.

I caught a big fat trout. Dad caught a bigger one. I caught three medium-sized ones. His were always bigger than anything I could catch. My complaining brought a smile to his brown, wrinkled face. "Ya ain't holdin' yer mouth right or somethin'." He said. "Takes time ta learn how to catch them r-e-a-l-l-y big ones."

"I'm learning," I said. My dog Ring gave me a warm, wet lick on the left side of my face.

"Well, son, it's gittin' late. It'll soon be chore time. Let's git on them donkeys and head fer home," he said. "From the looks of the clouds playin' 'round the tops of the mountain, we just might git a shower."

Blue and Jim headed home, their hooves disturbing the dust on the quiet road. A soft breeze from the west carried a fragrance of dampened dust on rain-struck grass.

It was the smell of a country childhood.

Henry (in straw hat) and Oris driving the team.

A Naked Impression

Henry and I were twelve years old and the best of friends. We got along because we enjoyed the same ignorance on many subjects—one of which was girls. It was a hot June Saturday in the summer of 1945 when Henry had his first lesson about how not to impress a girl.

At twelve years of age, we had not yet discovered girls were anything other than a pain. They giggled and laughed and acted silly.

Two weeks before we were to be released for the summer from the 'prison' known as Lincoln Junior High School, Laura Cranfield moved to town. Her father was the new bank president. Mrs. Andres had just given us our math assignment when the door opened. Mr. Kirk, the principal, ushered a girl into the room. There she stood, a vision of loveliness like never before seen – hair the color of ground cinnamon, eyes as blue as the sea. Right then and there, Henry fell in love. (The first of many 'true loves' in the years to come.)

The last two weeks of school dragged on and on

and on. At last, we were released from 'prison'. The lazy days of summer awaited us.

We spent the first afternoon of our new-found freedom swimming and making plans for the summer while Blue, my donkey, stood tied to a fence post close to the creek. I lived on a working ranch. Henry lived in town. As often as his mother would allow, and when I didn't have to work, he spent weekends at our place.

"Next Saturday, if Dad don't have sumthin' for me to do" I said, "let's look for magpie nests."

"I think Laura likes me," Henry said

"How do you know she likes you?"

"I saw her and her mother in the drugstore last night."

"You saw her in the drugstore and you think she l-i-k-e-s you? Man, you're nuts! That's the dumbest thing I've ever heard."

"Yeh. I could tell by the way she looked at me that she likes me."

"Fergit about that dumb girl," I said. "Do you wanna look for magpie nests on Saturday or not?"

"Yer jist mad 'cause she don't like you."

"I've got better things to do than moon around about some dumb girl," I said, and pushed his head under water.

We dived, swam, splashed, and ducked one another. We made plans to look for magpie nests, shoot prairie dogs, and ride donkeys, when I didn't have to work.

"I'm hungry," I said. "Let's go home and eat lunch."

"That's the smartest thing you've said in a month."

We climbed out of the water and up the bank. Did we ever get a shock! Sitting on a beautiful dappled-grey Arabian mare, Laura Cranfield was laughing and smiling.

"You boys sure are ugly without any clothes on."

The earth wouldn't swallow me, and Henry died in his wet tracks. With nothing available to cover our privates but our hands, we backed into the water. Henry, backing 500 miles per hour, tripped and fell backwards. While Henry splashed and choked, I tried to hide and keep from drowning. Laura sat her horse for a couple of minutes and continued to laugh. With a flip of her beautiful cinnamon-colored hair, she turned her horse and loped up the trail.

Henry was mad and embarrassed. He kicked a tree trunk. He didn't hurt the tree, but his big toe was a different matter. (It was much bigger for a very long time.)

Two weeks later, Henry and I, riding double on my donkey, Blue, heard a horse coming up behind us at a lope. It was Laura, the new-found love of Henry's life. "Hey guys, I see you have clothes on today," Laura called as she rode alongside us.

True to form, Henry tried to act all suave and relaxed. "Hi, Laura. That's a fine-looking horse. Sure is good to see you today."

"What a cute donkey," Laura said.

Nothing ticked me off more than someone calling Blue cute.

Trying to act all important, Henry asked, "You wanna ride her?"

"I like donkeys," Laura said. "Yes, I'd like to ride her."

We slid off Blue's back. Laura handed me the bridle reins to hold her horse. Henry gave her a leg-up, and she rode down the road a ways and back. "This is really a good donkey," she said.

We stood in the middle of the road and talked about the up-coming parade on Saturday. "I'd like to ride Blue in the parade and you could ride my mare," Laura said.

Henry blushed a deep red and said, "I gotta white donkey you could ride if you want to. It's a much better donkey than this one." Henry had a talent for revising the truth. Before I could get a word out of my mouth, Laura agreed and rode off 'into the sunset'. The truth of the matter was—the week before, I had traded Frankie Gadberry five red hens and a brown kid goat for a small white jenny donkey.

Saturday we met Laura at the Texaco service station. She traded her mare with Henry for my small white jenny donkey. Henry thought he had died and gone to heaven. He helped Laura up on the donkey before he stepped into the saddle on the Arabian mare.

Down the street they rode, Henry trying to act like Gene Autry and Laura sitting tall and composed as a rodeo queen.

The nerve center of our small town was the intersection of Sixth and Main Street. Right in the middle of the intersection, that white jenny donkey had a change of personality. She stopped dead in her donkey-tracks, squatted, slobbered, raised her tail, and brayed. Then she bucked. Taken by surprise, Laura abruptly became airborne. She landed on her back on the pavement. From her undignified position, she looked at Henry and let out a screech that was heard twenty miles away. The terror on her face right then and there convinced me that crazy ol' man Tillitson had sneaked up behind Henry with a hatchet.

So much for a young boy's trying to impress a young girl with a donkey.

Faded Blue Bonnet

In the fall of 1945 when I turned twelve, draft horses and mules were being slaughtered by the thousands. Before World War II, a few farmers and ranchers in our county purchased tractors, but horses and mules were still the main source of power on many farms. When my father married in 1931, he made the decision to continue farming with mules for so long as he was able to work.

After the war, the day of the draft animal started winding down. I remember that time as a sad illustration of the future.

In the early months of 1945, horses and mules began to swell the pens at the auctions. An increasing number of farmers did not want to keep their work stock.

On Saturdays, like red ants parading across a driveway, a never-ending line of trucks and trailers loaded with horses and mules arrived at the sale yards. About this same time, the demand for mink and fox furs took off like V-2 rockets. Many horses and mules went from the auction to the mink and fox farms to be used as meat to feed the mink and fox. A few found homes, but the majority went to the killers.

Some farmers did not want to see their horses and mules on the backs of people in the form of mink and fox coats. They disposed of their horses and mules at home. A trench or pit was dug with a slip or fresno. They led their horses and mules into the pit, shot them, and covered them with dirt.

Hog farmers were another limited market. They went to the auction, bought one or several horses or mules and took them to their operations. They drove into a pen full of hogs, unloaded the horses and mules, and shot them between the eyes. The hogs ate the carcasses where they fell.

Anna Tidwell was seventy years old and recently widowed. Mr. Tidwell had been a lover of good mules all his life. Anna also loved anything with long ears.

Shortly after Mr. Tidwell died, Anna showed up at our place one evening to talk with Dad. I, a very nosey kid sitting on the porch step, heard her tell Dad a neighbor was going to take his span of very old buckskin mules to the auction. She asked Dad if he would be interested in buying them to save them from the killers. Dad said we already had too many mules on the place.

Late Saturday afternoon, Anna stopped by the house and offered to pay Dad to go to the auction and haul her mules home. She paid $15 each for those old buckskin mules. That was the beginning of the first rescue effort I remember.

Anna existed on a very limited income. Her little farm, about half of it in pasture, could not support many mules. She went to work in town cleaning houses to earn extra money to buy feed. She bought old and crippled mules, good ones and not so good ones, and gave them a home until she could find a place for them.

During the first winter, she had to feed straw. We often saw her in her big black 1935 Buick as it 'putted' down the road with a bale of straw on the front and rear bumpers. She had so many mules she was spending her grocery money for feed. Dad got wind of the situation. Whenever he saw her carting home straw on the bumpers of her Buick, he hauled a load of hay over to her place.

Time moved on. Anna collected more mules.

The first summer I had any size to me and was strong enough to help in the hay, Dad said, "Son, take every fifth load o' bales over to Miz Anna's and you keep at it 'til her shed is full. Don't let her pay you for it. You hear me?"

Every summer after that, I hauled hay to Anna's. Everyday during winter, I rode my mule over to Anna's and fed her mules. Sometimes there were only a few, other times many. One Saturday morning in late

December my mother stopped her car alongside the road and counted 13 mules in Anna's pasture.

One morning Dad came in from the barn and asked Mom if she wanted to go to town with him to supervise his buying a new hat. He wore an old, battered brown Stetson hat in which no self-respecting scarecrow would be caught dead. Mom had nagged him for a long time to get a new one. (Finally, he grew tired of her nagging.) After an hour spent looking at hats, he kept the old one. To pacify Mom, he broke down and bought her an ice cream cone before they left town. (He was a big spender.)

Approaching Anna's place on the way home, they noticed Anna sitting by the water trough near the windmill. Dad turned into the lane and drove to the windmill. They found her sitting on a large block of wood, leaning against a corral post. Her cold, stiff hands held her faded blue bonnet neatly folded in her lap. *Anna had died.*

A Volcano on the River

Henry's father brought him out to spend several days at our place so his mother wouldn't go crazy with his lying around on the couch. (Teenage boys think it's their right to spend time on the couch in a horizontal position.)

By June, Henry and I already had aggravated fish in the creek so often they all left to safer water. Grandad Fletcher figured they probably went south to Mexico City or north to Alaska to escape our sorry attempts at fishin'. (Fish like a challenge, not the fumbling of two clumsy boys.)

With no fish in the creek, we needed something to occupy our time. We managed to escape Mom's eagle eye and the humiliation of having to pull weeds in the garden. Henry wanted to go up on the hill behind the barn to do some target shooting. I wanted to shoot magpies. We decided to ride the donkeys, Blue and Jiggs, over to the pond, go swimming and look for magpies on our way back to the house.

"Henry," I said, "what do you think about finishing

the volcano we started when we escaped from school for the summer? We can target practice and shoot magpies some other time."

"Sounds like a plan," Henry said.

"Go ask my mom for some matches while I catch Blue and Jiggs," I said.

Henry gave me a sour look. "Quit tellin' me what to do. I ain't your slave. You git the matches, and I'll go catch the donkeys."

"She'll give you the matches," I said. "Don't tell her why we want them, 'cause I ain't supposed to go down to the river."

In her mind, Mom knew Henry was a perfect boy, and she'd give him matches. When she looked at him, she saw a halo glowing around his head. (He could turn that halo on quick as a frog can blink.) The innocent look he turned on when he talked to my mother was an expression he practiced in front of a mirror.

I took a shortcut through the orchard and climbed over the fence. Blue and Jiggs, enjoying the warm summer day in the shade of a crooked cottonwood tree, looked at me as if to say, 'don't bother us'. I buckled my belt around Blue's neck and led her to the barn. Jiggs followed along like a big dog. I bridled them and tied them to the hitch-rack.

Henry came around the corner of the barn and said, "Your mother didn't even ask me what I wanted with matches."

"Told ya so."

"I'm riding Jiggs, so that leaves you with Blue," I said.

"You rode Jiggs yesterday."

"I don't care. They're my donkeys. You ride Blue and quit belly-achin' or walk. Don't make a dime's difference to me."

"Sometimes you're a real jerk."

I laughed and said, "Let's go to the shop and pick up a hatchet and some wire."

"What we need wire for?" Henry asked.

"How you figure we're going to tie the top of the sticks together without wire? Sometimes you ask the dumbest questions."

"You really think you're smart, don't cha?"

Dad's shiny new hatchet, hanging on the wall, begged us to take it instead of the old rusty one in a five-gallon bucket.

Henry said, "Oris, you take the wire and I'll carry the hatchet."

"Why should you take the hatchet instead of me?"

"Because, if we run into ol' Elmer Tillitson, you're too chicken to scalp the old buzzard. I'm not."

We mounted the donkeys and rode around behind the henhouse and across the south pasture so Mom couldn't see us heading for the river. When we reached the county road, we saw Jack Hull coming our way. We waited for him. Jack was two years older than we were. He was a 'neat' sorta guy. He rode a fine-looking black saddle horse. He smoked a pack of Lucky Strikes a day, and stayed out at night on the weekends until after one-o'clock in the morning.

"What you guys doin' with that hatchet and balin' wire?" Jack asked.

Henry, always the big-shot, said, "We're goin' down to the river. I'm gonna show Oris how to finish a volcano we started to build the other day. You wanna come with us?

"Why not? If I go home, my ol' man'll have me muckin' out the barn. I sure as heck don't wanna spend the rest o' the day shovelin' cow manure."

Three boys, two donkeys, one horse, one shiny hatchet, and a hank of baling wire headed for the river.

Arriving at the river, Jack tied his horse to a small cottonwood tree.

"Henry," I said. "Let's turn these donkeys loose so they can graze. They'll not wander off."

Jack walked around the volcano Henry and I had started. He wasn't impressed. "You roosters call this a volcano? It looks like somethin' my little sister built. It's way too small, should be a lot taller 'n bigger around at the base. On top o' that, the hole in the top ain't big enough to let smoke out."

Henry bristled. "What makes you an expert on building volcanoes?"

"Me 'n my cousin, Sonny, have been buildin'

volcanos ever since we was in the sixth grade."

The three of us looked for a place free of weeds and dead grass. "Here we go," Jack said. "Oris, you 'n Henry dig a hole about as big around as a wash tub and eight or ten inches deep and fill it with dry grass and leaves and put some dead sticks on top. That's what we'll light and use to make smoke when we git this here thing finished."

"Okay," I said.

"Then, you guys cut a bunch o' straight willow poles about six feet long and big around as a broomstick. Make sure they're green. That way they won't burn when we light the fire. I saw a bucket in the bar ditch back up the road. I'll go git it. We'll use it to mix mud for the outside o' the volcano. That way the smoke'll go out the hole in the top and not seep out the cracks between the sticks."

Henry and I took turns cutting willows. We stacked a big pile next to the fire pit. "Hey, Jack," Henry called. "How many of these dumb poles do we need?"

"Keep choppin'. We'll need a bunch more."

Henry and I took turns chopping and dragging, dragging and chopping poles.

"Okay, guys. You got 'nough poles. Henry and me'll stick a pole in the ground. Oris you hold it in place while we put one on the other side. We want ta make it kinda like an Indian teepee. When we git four poles up, I'll tie the tops together. Then, we'll start putting the rest in place. We'll alternate sides. That way it'll hold itself up and not fall off to one side."

The volcano began to take shape. Jack stepped back, looked at it, and said, "We're almost done. It's lookin' good! Oris, cut five poles about ten inches shorter. When we put 'em in place, I'll wire 'em so there's a hole we can use to put wood on the fire inside."

"Oris, you mix mud in that bucket. Don't make it too stiff, and slap it on the volcano while Henry 'n me have a smoke. You don't smoke. So, while we smoke, you do the mud thing. That way the work won't stop.

"No way, man. If you guys stop, I stop."

We sat on an old cottonwood log while Jack and Henry enjoyed their smokes.

Jack finished his cigarette and flipped the butt into the river. We watched it float away. "Okay, guys. Let's finish this volcano of all volcanoes. It's gittin' close to chore time. If I'm late doin' chores, my old man'll choke on his tongue, and he'll ground me for a thousand years."

We mixed and plastered mud, finished the volcano, and washed the mud off our hands in the river. Jack walked around the volcano and then sat on the log. "Guys," he said. "This looks more like a teepee than a volcano."

We laughed.

Henry said, "We got time to light the fire under

this thing and watch it smoke before chore time, don't we?"

Jack looked at his dollar pocket watch and said, "Sure. Why not?"

Henry scratched a match on his belt buckle. He stuck the lighted match in the hole at the bottom of the volcano and touched it to the dry grass and leaves. The small flame caught the grass. It flared to a fast burn. We put more dry wood on the fire. Smoke curled out of the hole in the top. Not a breeze anywhere. The smoke rose straight up. We had a volcano. Jack said, "Ain't you guys glad I come along in time ta help ya build this thing?"

The picture of that volcano sending smoke to the clouds that summer day in 1947 is as clear in my mind today as it was sixty-some years ago.

"I gotta go. See you guys later." Jack untied his horse and loped up the trail toward the county road.

I gathered a bunch of dried grass and leaves and laid them close to the fire hole. "I'll put this stuff here so we'll have it to start a fire next time."

"Sounds like a plan," Henry said.

We jumped on Blue and Jiggs. "I'll race ya to the county road," Henry said.

"You're on!" I kicked Jiggs in the ribs, and he trotted past Blue and Henry.

"It's my turn to ride Jiggs," Henry said.

"No way, man. You rode Blue comin', and you'll

ride her goin' home."

We reached the county road and were about a quarter of a mile from the river when we met ol' Elmer Tillitson in his rattle-trap of a pickup. He applied the brakes and skidded to a stop. The dust settled—he glared at me like he did every time he saw me. "Henry," he said. "You jist come from the river. What's that smoke down there all about?"

We looked back towards the river and saw an angry cloud of smoke boiling above the cottonwood trees.

Henry, always the one to make himself look good, said, "Oris smoked a cigarette. Fire must have started when he threw the butt away."

I panicked! My heart started beating a thousand beats a second. I wanted to choke the life out of him.

Three other vehicles came 'flying' down the road and stopped behind Elmer's pickup. Dad and Grandad Fletcher jumped out of Dad's pickup. "What's goin' on, Elmer?" Dad asked.

Elmer gave me a look of utter disgust and said, "Henry says Oris started a fire down there in the dry brush. Charles, you gotta get a handle on that boy."

Grandad Fletcher, not one to get excited, said, "Elmer, why don't ya go off some- wheres by yerself and do us all a favor and have a stroke."

By this time, a crowd had gathered to watch the fire.

"I tell ya," Elmer said. "That fire is gonna burn all

along the river."

"That's a hot fire but it ain't goin' far," Earl Brooks said. "It's just burning that short strip along the north bank. It'll burn itself out 'fore long."

The men stood around in a group and watched the fire and smoke. In about an hour, it began to show signs of burning out. "Nothing to do here," Mr. Cathcart said. "I'm goin' home and milk that old red cow and call it a day." The neighbors got in their vehicles, turned around in the middle of the road and followed Mr. Cathcart.

Dad and Grandad were the last to leave. Dad gave me a look that said, "We'll talk about this later."

Grandad placed his right hand on Dad's shoulder and, thinking I couldn't hear said, "Charles, it might be a good idea not ta say much ta the boy's mother 'bout this. Whatcha think?"

At supper that night, Dad told Mom about the fire along the river.

The next day Henry and I snuck off to the river. We tied the donkeys to a fence post and walked to where the fire had burned. The ground was covered with black and grey ashes. The volcano was still standing, none the worse for the fire. The dried leaves and grass I placed on the ground next to the fire-hole in the volcano must have somehow caught fire.

One snowy Saturday morning that winter, Henry

ORIS GEORGE

and I fired up the volcano and watched the smoke
disappear into the slow-falling snow.

Sounds like a Plan

I can still hear my Dad's parting words, "Oris. Keep an eye on things and stay out o' trouble. Ya hear?" Of course, I'd stay out of trouble. Did he think I was a little kid or what?

My parents and my little brothers, Ralph and Eddie, had gone to the city for three days and left me home alone to do chores and look after things. Had Dad known what was going to happen while they were away, he never would have gone.

The dust no sooner settled when a car came 'fogging' up the lane and skidded to a stop at the porch door. Henry stuck his head out the front passenger window and said, "My Dad brought me out to see if I could spend the weekend with you while he and Mom are out of town."

"Sure," I said. "It's okay."

Henry reached into the back seat for a small gray metal suitcase that contained a change of clothes. "Thanks, Dad," he said.

"You boys take care. Henry, your mother will come

123

get you Sunday night." He waved and drove back down the lane. I neglected to tell him my folks had gone to the city.

So, there we stood—two thirteen-year old boys (almost fourteen), with the weekend before us and no one to tell us what to do—how to do it—when to do it. Luck was on our side.

I slapped Henry on the back and said, "My folks are gone for three days. There's no one here to tell us what to do. I like the idea already."

"Neat-O," Henry said, and he pumped the air with his right fist. "What's the plan, dummy?"

"I'll 'dummy you', you horses' rear end." I slugged him in the gut and headed for the barn.

Henry spent a lot of time at our place and knew what chores needed to be done. "I'll feed the mules and bring the milk cows in from pasture while you feed the calves and rabbits," I said. "Then, we'll milk those two yellow Jersey cows."

I opened the barn door. Jack and Joe, Dad's big gray mules, walked to their individual stalls. I put their halters on, tied them to the feed manger, and poured two quarts of oats into their grain boxes. They were content as they chomped their oats.

The cows were standing at the pasture gate. "Come on, cows," I said as I opened the sagging wooden gate. "Time's wastin'. We ain't got all day, so hurry along there."

Henry milked Daisy. I milked Ruth.

"Watch this," I called to Henry. Two cats assumed their customary positions behind Ruth. I squirted a stream of milk at them. They caught the milk in their mouths, then licked their front paws and cleaned their faces.

Henry finished milking Daisy and placed the three-legged milk stool next to the wall. As he walked by me carrying a bucket half-full of milk, I said, "Hey, manure head, look at this."

"What?"

"This." I squirted a stream of milk catching him right in the kisser. With the back of his right hand, he tried to wipe the milk off his face.

"You sorry piece of crap!" He dumped his bucket of warm milk in my face and streaked for the door.

I darn near fell off the milk stool. Scrambling to my feet, I tried to clear warm sticky milk out of my eyes.

Holding a half-full bucket of warm milk, I took off after Henry. As he reached the door, I sloshed my bucket of milk down his neck.

He stopped—he turned around—he glared at me. His face grew redder than an overripe summer tomato. Out of his mouth rushed words so foul they gave off a powerful stench.

"What's the matter, ya little sissy?" I said. "Can't ya handle a little warm milk?"

For several seconds, we stood glaring at each other. The red drained from his face. I laughed. Then he laughed.

I turned the cows into the corral.

At the watering trough, we washed milk off our faces. Henry called me a twelve-letter word.

"Come on, Henry. Let's go to the house and heat water for a bath."

"Sounds like a plan to me."

I built a fire in the cookstove while Henry filled Mom's copper wash boiler with water.

"You started this crap," Henry said. "So, I get a bath first."

"Okay with me."

While the water was heating, we stripped off our cruddy shirts and jeans. Clad only in our shorts, we sat on a bench on the back porch. (Henry grumbled and complained.) The water finally reached a boil.

"It's too hot in this kitchen to take a bath," I said. "Let's put the tub on the back porch." The kitchen door opened onto the porch which was screened on three sides. A screened door opened off the porch to the backyard and driveway.

(No bathroom or running water in our house—we always used one of Mom's wash tubs for a bathtub.)

I dumped three buckets of hot water into the tub. Henry added cold water until he was satisfied the water wasn't too hot or too cold for his 'tenderness'.

He removed his shorts and stepped into the tub. He stood naked as a proverbial jaybird.

We heard a car pull into the yard.

"Oh, crap." Henry said.

Faster than a screaming bullet, I stepped back into the kitchen and shut and locked the door. Henry jumped out of the tub. His feet were wet. He slipped. He fell. The kitchen door was locked. He had no way to escape. No way was I going to unlock that door. Henry panicked.

"Open that #+^*% door," he shouted. "I'm gonna kill you." He called me a fifteen-letter word.

"If you say 'pretty please', I'll open the door." He continued to cuss.

I heard a car door slam. Henry heard it.

In his birthday suit—with no place to hide— someone coming up the walk to open the screen door, for once in his sheltered 'city-boy' life, Henry had no control of the situation. "Purty please open the door," he begged.

I opened the door. (He didn't even say 'thank you' as he streaked across the kitchen and found safety in the broom closet.)

Our neighbor, Mrs. Cathcart, opened the screen door.

"How are you, Mrs. Cathcart?" I asked innocently.

"I'm well. Thank you," she said, and looked at the galvanized tub full of water. Her eyes followed the wet footprints across the porch floor.

"Is your mother here?"

"No, Ma'am. My parents are gone for a few days."

"Well then, tell her I stopped by, and have her call me." She peered at the wet footprints and tub of water as she turned and went back out the door to her car.

"You can come out now, sissy," I said.

Henry opened the closet door a crack to see if it was safe to come out. (He didn't trust me.) "One of these days, I'm gonna drive a rusty nail through your stupid head." He was still hot under the collar. (He didn't have clothes on, so he had no collar.)

By the time we finished our baths, dressed and emptied the bath water, Henry was laughing.

"I'm bored clear to my ears. We gotta find something ta do," Henry said. "We can't sit here and swat mosquitoes all night. Let's take your Dad's truck and split for town. I'll spring for a couple of burgers, and we'll take in the show. Whatcha say?"

"Can't do that," I said.

"Why not? Your ol' man won't know. Come on, let's go."

Off to town we went, bouncing along the county road, laughing like we owned good sense. I pulled into the parking lot at *Murphy's Poor Boy*. Goldie Martin, a foxy red-headed carhop, took our order for two burgers, potato chips, and two Orange Crushes. As she walked away, she glanced back over her right shoulder at Henry.

"Did you see the way she looked at me?" Henry said. "I think she likes me."

"Man, what's wrong with you? She's eighteen years old, almost old enough to be your mother. Besides, you won't be fourteen for another two months. You're one dumb horse's rear end."

"Nothin' wrong with me. I like foxy girls—they like me."

Parked next to Tony Gillespie's new blue 1947 Dodge coupe, Dad's old black pickup looked as out of place as a box turtle on Aunt Maude's fancy lace tablecloth.

Goldie was all smiles as she placed a loaded tray in the window of Tony's car. Tony looked at Goldie, showed her his Frank Sinatra smile, and said, "You wanna go for a ride after you get off work?"

"Sure thing. I get off at seven."

"See ya then," Tony said.

Henry leaned out the window. "Hey, Tony, how many miles ya got on that classy car now?"

Tony looked at the speedometer and said, "569 miles."

Henry tried to keep the one-sided conversation going. He soon ran out of questions and anything to say.

Goldie deposited our tray in the window and said, "Here you go. That'll be one dollar and sixty cents."

Henry handed her two dollars and twenty-five cents. He said, "Keep the change." She said a polite 'thank-you' and walked away. She waved at Tony as she went to wait on a car loaded with teenagers.

A limp-fish look attached itself to Henry's face as he watched her walk away.

Man. She didn't even give you the time of day," I said.

We parked the pickup on Seventh Street and walked two blocks to the Rialto Theater. The line to get into the movie, *Duel in the Sun*, stretched for half a block. Tickets cost a dollar and a half each—popcorn and a candy bar another twenty cents.

Roy Rogers and Dale Evans were no longer our favorite movie actors. We grew up a lot that night. Jennifer Jones remained our favorite until Marilyn Monroe starred in *The Seven Year Itch*.

After the show, Tony Gillespie and Goldie asked us if we wanted to drag Main. We followed them and seven other cars down Main Street to First Street and back to Fifteenth Street.

On the way out of town, we stopped at Brickle's Texaco filling station. Henry bought a Coke and a pack of Pall Mall cigarettes. I bought a Grape Nehi and a Hershey bar.

We walked into the kitchen as the mantle clock in the hall struck midnight. I scratched a match on my pant leg and lit the kerosene lamp that sat in the middle of the kitchen table. Grandma Fletcher had come by and placed a cherry pie on the counter. While I cut the pie in half and dished it out on two plates, Henry brought a pitcher of milk from the icebox.

Henry laughed and said, "Man. This is the life. We took your Dad's pickup to town, had a burger, went to the show, drug Main. Now we have all the cherry pie we can eat before we go to bed. Life can't get any better than this."

Long before the sun thought about showing it's face in the east, two roosters with their scratchy, choking crowing took turns announcing the coming day. Henry covered his head with a pillow and said, "Let's drown those $*#% roosters. You can tell your Mom coyotes ate 'em and you can buy her an alarm clock." (Henry wasn't one to get up early.)

We were finishing chores when Grandad walked into the barn. "Well, men," he said. "How goes life this fine Saturrdee morning? Ain't ya a wee bit late doin' chores?"

"Mr. Fletcher. I tried to get Oris up. He said his folks were gone and they'd not know what time he did chores." (Henry was a master at telling a lie that would fit the moment.)

"Henry, I didn't know ya was here."

"Oris, yer Grandma sent me over here ta bring ya ta breakfast. You two over-grown pups hop in the car, and we'll go see if there's 'nough grub fer two hungry boys."

"My goodness," Grandma said. "It's good to see you two. Sit down and we'll have breakfast. Oris, did you find the pie I left last evening?"

Henry couldn't wait to run his mouth and said, "Yes, Ma'am. We were over at the pond until after dark." The fib slid off his tongue so smooth even I almost believed him. "Mrs. Fletcher, you sure make a delicious cherry pie. It's better than the ones my mother makes."

"Why thank you, Henry."

"Grandma," I said. "Thanks for breakfast. It was lots better than the Puffed Wheat we'd o' had at home."

Henry, always the one to be so polite he stunk, jumped up to help Grandma clear the table. While he was rinsing dishes, Grandad leaned over and whispered in my left ear, "Last night I saw yer Dad's pickup parked on Seventh Street. How ya figure it got there?" He stood up, tossled my hair, and said, "You boys ready ta go home? I'm headed fer town. I'll drop ya off ta yer place."

Grandad and Henry talked all the way home. I never said a word. All I could think about was what would happen when Dad and Mom got home.

Grandad stopped at the barn. "Thank you, Mr. Fletcher, for the ride and breakfast." Henry said. "Holler if you need us to help with anything today." Grandad honked the horn and drove away.

"Henry," I said. "We're in trouble. Grandad saw Dad's pickup in town last night, and he knows we were late doing chores this morning."

"So what. You think he'll tell your Dad? I don't think so. Forget it. If your Dad does find out, we'll think of something. I'm bored. What we gonna do today?"

"I've got a box of .22 shells," I said. "What say we go out behind the barn and do some target practice?"

"Sounds like a plan."

We scrounged up a bunch of tin cans and lined them up for targets. We flipped a quarter to see who got the first shot. Henry won. He said, "I'll keep shootin' 'til I miss. Then you shoot 'til you miss. Okay?"

Henry was a good shot with a .22 rifle and he hit and rolled ten cans before he missed. He wouldn't have missed then if the can wasn't rolling down hill. I hit the first can and rolled it with 13 shots before I missed. In less than an hour, we were out of shells and decided to ride donkeys over to the pond.

We rode along the dusty road in the gentle sunshine of a soft summer day. A flock of red-winged blackbirds, singing as they perched and hopped around in the cattails, added their contribution to a gentle, slow day. I tied Jim to a willow bush. Henry turned Blue loose. She didn't need to be tied. She'd stay close to Jim.

We skipped smooth rocks across the glass-like surface of the water. Henry said, "I think I'll be a baseball pitcher."

"Make up your mind, man. Last week you were gonna be a lawyer."

"I think I'll pitch for the New York Yankees. Babes like baseball players."

"I was beginning to worry about you. It's almost noon and you ain't mentioned a girl or girls yet. You sick or something?"

Henry plopped down on the grass and lit a cigarette. He said, "If we left now, we could make it to your Grandad's about dinner time."

As the morning slipped away, I forgot about Grandad seeing the pickup in town. Now, as I thought about it, for some reason, I wasn't worried. "Okay," I said. "Let's go."

Grandad met us at the gate. He looked at his Rockford pocket watch and said, "It appears you two pups are lookin' fer a free meal. If that's the case, ya timed it 'bout right. Tie them donkeys ta the fence and git washed-up."

The comforting smell of fresh-baked bread drifted through the kitchen door.

Henry wasn't satisfied with washing his hands. He wasted another five minutes messing with his hair. "Hurry up, Henry," I said. "Whatcha doing, trying to make yourself look pretty? It ain't gonna work. You're just plain ugly." He slugged me on my right shoulder.

"Now, boys," Grandma said. "Come on in here

and sit down, and I'll fill your plates."

For Henry, eating was a serious business. After he inhaled the food Grandma had piled on his plate, he said, "Mrs. Fletcher, you are the best cook I know. Would you share your recipe for this tasty blueberry cobbler with my Mother? It's the best blueberry cobbler I've ever had."

I almost 'puked' listening to him.

"Why thank you, Henry. What a sweet thing to say. I'll talk to your mother about the recipe."

I went into the pantry and wrote a note to Grandma. "Thank you for dinner. I love you." I signed it 'Oris' and left it on the flour sack.

Grandad had shouldered his shovel and gone to change irrigation water.

As always, Henry was in a hurry. We mounted the donkeys and headed home. Henry heeled Jim, trying to get him to walk faster. (Jim knew more about young boys than young boys knew about donkeys.) He promptly lay down in the middle of the road. Henry shot over Jim's head and landed on his belly in the gravel. He staggered to his feet and had some colorful descriptive words for Jim. (Good ol' Jim ignored him.)

Henry's face began to acquire a deep shade of red— like a tomato.

Jim had no intention of standing up. He sat on his haunches like a big dog.

Henry pulled hard on the reins and said, "Git up, you stupid jackass." Jim's neck stretched. He didn't budge.

"Take his bridle off and leave him there," I said.

Henry yanked the bridle off. He swung up behind me. (We proceeded on down the road to the tune of many new cuss words Henry invented to suit the situation.)

When we arrived at the barn, Jim was trotting right behind us. That crazy donkey didn't want to be left behind so he trotted to catch up with Blue. Henry was still 'ticked'.

We turned the donkeys into the corral, and I said, "Henry, let's go to the house and listen to the radio 'til time to do chores."

"Sounds like a plan," he said.

By chore time, the radio battery was growing weak. I knew Mom would be upset because we had run the battery down.

After chores, we washed up and found something to eat.

"Man, I'm bored," Henry said. We gotta find something to do. Let's wait 'til dark then take your ol' man's pickup and go to town for a while. I'll spring for two Orange Crushes. We can drag Main a couple of times and be back before too late. Whatcha think?"

"I don't think so. Grandad said he saw Dad's pickup in town last night, and he might tell Dad. If he sees the pickup in town again, I'll be in deep trouble. Besides, my folks trust me to take care of things while they're gone."

"Look at it this way. Did they tell you not to drive the pickup? You drive all over this ranch. What's wrong with going to town?"

"Dad's never let me drive in town. The reason he taught me to drive in the first place is in case of an accident, I could drive to the hospital or something."

"Come on, man. Don't be such a wimp. Nothin's gonna happen. What are the chances of your Grandad being in town again tonight? It's Saturday night. We'll pick up two Orange Crushes at *Murphy's Poor Boy*. Then we'll drag Main Street. We can stop at Ott's Candy Store and check out the foxy babes that work the soda fountain. Your ol' man'll never know."

"Okay. Let's go," I said.

"You got a T-shirt I can borrow? I didn't bring one with me."

We changed into white T-shirts and penny-loafers. Henry rolled a pack of Lucky Strikes in the left sleeve. He fussed a good five minutes with his hair, trying to get it perfect.

"You gonna spend all night combing your hair? You might as well quit messin' with it 'cause it still looks like a head o' rotten cabbage." I dodged the shoe he threw.

About a mile outside of town, Henry said, "How

about lettin' me drive? Your Dad'll not find out." I pulled over to the side of the road, jumped out, and ran around the front of the pickup. Henry slid behind the steering wheel. "Here we go," he said, as he ground the gears trying to shift into first."

The pickup parted the pleasant smell of new mown hay as we drove through the soft summer evening.

Once inside the city limits, Henry honked at every car we met.

The parking lot at *Murphy's Poor Boy* was full of cars loaded with teenagers, and more teenagers standing around, guys and girls flirting from car-to-car or just yelling or visiting. Henry found a spot right at the front door. Sonny Hilton pulled in beside us. He hollered to Henry, "What you doin' drivin' that pickup?"

Henry leaned out the window and said (loud enough for everyone to hear), "Oris's dad won't let him drive, but he lets me drive it."

"That's good. You wanna follow me and we'll drag Main?"

"Sounds like a plan," Henry said. He started the pickup and backed out to follow Sonny.

Henry honked, waved and whistled at every 'girl' on both sides of the street.

We drug Main a couple of times, then followed Sonny. We parked on a side street and walked a block to *Ott's Candy Store*. The place was packed with talking, laughing, noisy teenagers enjoying Saturday night.

Tony waved us over to sit with him and Goldie.

A cheerful waitress with long, blonde, cascading hair made her way to our table. She smiled a disarming smile and said, "May I take your orders?"

Henry looked at her. Lightning shattered the heavens—thunder galloped across the face of the earth—the wind stood still—his eyes popped six inches out of his head. He was in love like never before.

Goldie giggled and said, Henry, put your eyes back in your head."

Tony laughed, slapped Henry on the back and said, "Take a deep breath, man. Your face is turning purple and your tongue's hangin' out!"

The cause of Henry's turmoil asked again. May I take your orders?"

In less time than it takes a mosquito to buzz an ear, Henry was in charge of the situation. He smiled a smile that went clear around behind his ears and said, "I'm buying. Five large, chocolate marshmallow milk shakes."

"That's my man," Tony said.

The newfound love of Henry's life wrote the order on the little white pad in her left hand. She smiled at Henry—turned and glided away.

"That's one good-looking babe," Henry said.

Sonny laughed and said, "You got that right."

"Be right back," Henry said. "Oris 'n me got something to do." He motioned for me to follow him.

139

We went outside and stood on the sidewalk away from the front window.

"You gotta help me out," Henry said. "I'm a dollar and a half short. Don't have enough to pay for the milk shakes."

"That's not my problem. You got yourself in this mess."

"Come on, man! I'll pay ya back."

I opened my billfold and found a dollar. My pockets gave up seventy-six cents.

"Thanks, man," Henry said, and he slugged my right shoulder. We went back to the table.

The reason for Henry's living arrived with our milk shakes in their frosty glasses. She handed Henry the ticket. He counted out the money, making sure she understood the extra thirty cents was a tip. "Thank you," she said. As she turned to leave, she smiled at Sonny. Sonny winked at her.

"Whatcha say we finish these milk shakes?" Tony said. "Then let's drag Main a couple o' times before we head for the dance at the Grange Hall."

"Sounds like a plan," Henry said.

We finished our milk shakes. Tony and Sonny each left a dime for a tip.

We followed Sonny and ended up fourth in a line of seven cars dragging Main. At the west end of Main Street, Tony turned south on Randall Street and headed for the Grange Hall. Henry followed.

"What are you doing?" I asked.

"Dummy. We're goin' to the dance. What do you think I'm doing?"

"Ain't no way, man, we're going to the dance." I said.

"Why not?"

"You know as well as me. We shouldn't be driving this pickup, let alone go to a dance without our folks' permission."

"Are you a wimp tonight, or what? Our folks are out of town—they'll never know. Quit being such a wimp."

We parked next to Tony's car.

"Henry. We're not going to the dance." I said.

Tony hollered, "You guys gonna sit in that pickup all night? The dance's inside."

Henry hollered back, "I guess not. Sissy pants Oris is afraid his 'mamma' will find out he's gone to a dance." He started the pickup and drove off the parking lot. He was ticked and didn't say a word until we were out of town headed home on the county road.

"You make me sick! You're the biggest wimp I've ever seen! Right now, we could be at the dance having a good time. But no! You're afraid your 'mamma' will get mad. She ain't gonna find out anyway. I heard that foxy waitress tell Goldie she would be there later tonight. I know she likes me. I could tell the way she looked at me. Why do you always have to do everything right?"

He was mad and driving way too fast.

"Do you think you are a big shot or what? That chick is eighteen years old. You won't be fourteen 'til October. You'll be in the ninth grade this fall, and she'll be a senior in high school. The only reason she knew you were there tonight is because you had to show off and leave her a big tip."

"Shut your trap. What do you know anyway—Mr. Goody Two Shoes?"

"Slow down!" I said.

The words had not escaped the inside of the pickup when Henry turned the corner. Going too fast in the loose gravel, the pickup slid off the road and hit a telephone pole. My head connected with the windshield. Henry's door flew open—he came to a sliding halt on his stomach—the pickup stuttered, coughed and died in a cloud of dust.

The lights on the pickup had gone out. I fumbled around and found the door handle. I called to Henry. I couldn't see him in the dark! "Are you okay?" I heard him coughing. My head hurt. My nose was bleeding all over my shirt. I stumbled around behind the pickup and tripped over Henry. He was sitting trying to cough his socks up.

"You okay?" I asked.

"Hell no! I'm not okay! My mouth is full of dirt and this dust is choking me. Are you okay?"

A car came around the corner. It stopped as the

headlights flooded the scene.

A man's voice said, "What happened here? Are you boys okay?" The voice belonged to Ben Canterbury, the county sheriff. He helped Henry to his feet. Henry was a little wobbly but okay. "You boys go sit in my car. I want to see what I can do about stopping Oris' nosebleed." He handed me a handkerchief and said, "Hold this under your nose. You have a bloody nose and the grandfather of all bumps on your forehead. Are you sure you're okay?"

"Yes, sir. I'm okay."

"What are you boys doing driving around at night? I know neither one of you has got a driver's license."

"We been to town," I said.

Sheriff Canterbury, huffing in his mustache, walked around the pickup. He said, "The front end is all messed up. It will have ta be towed. Here's what I'll do, Oris. I'll take you home and see how your dad wants to go about getting his pickup home."

I swallowed a lump in my throat as big as a baseball and said, "My folks aren't home. They won't be home until tomorrow night."

"Okay then. I'll run you by your Granddad Fletcher's."

For once in his life, Henry didn't have a thing to say.

"You know something? You two boys, between you, don't have as many brains as a turtle has feathers. You

143

could a done yourselves a world o' hurt." The silence in the sheriff's car was as quiet as math class when Mrs. Carter asks for a volunteer to work a problem on the blackboard.

When we topped the hill and looked down at our house, I stopped breathing. The house was lit up. A soft glow from kerosene lamps spilled out of every window.

We drove into the yard and found Dad's car and Grandad Fletcher's pickup parked in the yard.

Dad, Mom and Grandad and Grandma Fletcher were standing on the porch steps. Mom and Dad had come home a day early.

Sheriff Canterbury said to Dad, "Charles, look what I found along with your wrecked pickup."

My heart dropped to my feet. My stomach filled with butterflies. I knew I was in serious trouble.

Elmer's Bull

Oris, what have you done now?" Mom asked.

"Nothin', Mom."

"I know better," she said. "You've got that innocent look all over your grubby face. When I see 'that look', I know you're trying to cover up some atrocity that only you can find to do!"

At 15 years old, I wasn't sure what the word 'atrocity' meant, so I figured I was home free. It would be a disappointment to Mom if she thought I didn't know the meaning of the word. (She was always telling anyone who would listen how smart I was.) She'd say, "Oris knows everything. No one can tell him a solitary thing." I didn't want to upset her by admitting there was something I didn't know, even if it was the meaning of some unimportant word. Little did I know that for the rest of my life, on occasion, that hot summer in 1948 would bubble to the surface of my memory.

Henry and I had just walked into the house. We had been gone for two days and nights working for Grandad Fletcher. I was smiling and thinking of the prank we had pulled on ol' Elmer Tillitson. Mom always thought the worst when I'd been away from home for a few days. She knew Henry was perfect in every way. He had an infectious personality. He was tall, athletic, with thick blonde hair, bottomless blue eyes, and a smile that Clark Gable would die for. He could charm the stripes off a zebra. In Mom's eyes, Henry could do no wrong. (Little did she know.)

If Henry was so perfect, why did she worry so much when we were together?

Summer hit full swing.

Henry's parents, not wanting to spend the hot summer in town, had gone to visit family in northern Montana. They planned on being gone most of the summer. Henry pitched a fit and didn't want to go with them. My mother suggested Henry stay with us. Dad offered to pay him to help around the ranch. On days we didn't work, which wasn't often, we fished, went swimming, shot magpies and prairie dogs. That is, if Mom didn't force us to do hard, humiliating labor, like hoeing weeds in her vegetable garden.

After the hay was hauled and stowed in the barn, Dad told us we could take a few days off. We decided to go fishing. Dad lived to fish He always emptied the coffee grounds at the foot of an apple tree in the southeast corner of the garden. Hungry worms ate those coffee grounds and grew big and fat. (While he was baiting the hook, the fish would jump right up on the creek bank and fight to see who'd get the fat, juicy worm.)

"Henry. Dig some worms while I get the fishing poles."

Each of us, with a pole over the right shoulder, started down the hot, dusty road. Grandad Fletcher, in his rattling 1927 Model A Ford coupe, came chugging up the road in a cloud of dust. The Model A clattered to a stop.

"Where ya two boys off to?" Grandad asked (as if the fishing poles weren't a dead give away).

"We're gonna catch a mess of fish for supper," Henry answered.

Grandad smiled, scratched his nose and said, "Ya boys have annoyed them fish in the creek so often this summer they've gone ta safer waters. They probably went north ta Canada or Maine ta 'scape yer pathetic attempts at fishin'. Fish like a challenge, not the fumblin' o' two young boys."

"Grandpa, come and go with us," I said.

"I can't do that, boy. Got lots ta do taday."

"Mr. Fletcher," Henry said, "we'll catch a big'n for you."

"Thanks, boys," Grandad said. He put the Model A in gear and rattled away.

Henry picked up a rock and threw it at a magpie sitting on a fence post. He missed. A dust devil danced across the road in front of us. A hawk circled overhead as we walked on down the dusty road. Just before we

ORIS GEORGE

got to the creek, we heard a car coming behind us. It was Grandad. The brakes squealed and the Model A ground to a halt. It backfired and blew a perfect smoke ring when Grandad turned the key off.

"Well, men," Grandad said. "With no fish in the crick, and ya needin' somethin' ta do 'sides go swimmin' these few days, Oris's dad says ya can goof off. Instead a wastin' yer time tryin' ta catch fish that ain't anywheres near, hows about comin' ta work fer me? Got fence needs fixin', some hay ta haul, and a chicken coop what's in need of a good cleanin'. The good part o' this deal is all ya can eat three times a day, and ice cream every night. Ya can sleep in the twin beds upstairs. Out o' the kindness o' my big heart, I'll pay ya each four dollars a day."

With not a penny to my name and a new show at the movies I wanted to see, I said, "Okay, Grandad. Sounds good to me. Whatcha say, Henry?"

Henry thought for a few seconds before he answered. (The only thing Henry could ever make a quick decision about was how much pie he could eat.) I could see his pea-brain thinking, 'If I hold out for a few minutes, maybe Mr. Fletcher will offer four dollars and twenty-five cents.'

"Well, boys, I gotta go. So how does my offer sound ta ya?"

Henry looked at me and then at Grandad. "I will be more than happy to help you out, Mr. Fletcher."

"Good. Jump in. We'll take them fishin' poles back ta the house and ya can pick up a change o' clothes. I already talked ta Oris's dad. He said it's okay."

We worked the rest of the day and collected our first bowl of ice cream.

Grandad rousted us out at 5:00 a.m. Grandma fed us a hearty breakfast of eggs, ham, biscuits and milk.

"Henry, drink your milk," Grandma said. (Henry didn't get along with milk. He wanted coffee.)

"Oris, I gotta run inta town this mornin'," Grandad said. "You boys stop at the shop an' pick up a posthole digger, two shovels, the wire stretchers, a hammer and a can of staples. Go over ta the fence 'tween me 'n Elmer's and replace them five rotten posts before Elmer blows a gut." Elmer was Grandad's nearest neighbor. They shared a fence.

We harnessed Buck and Jack, Grandad's buckskin mules, and hitched them to the Bains wagon. We drove around to the shop and loaded the tools. Henry started around the back of the wagon and almost collided with Tom, Grandma's big pet tom turkey. (Ol' Tom was a sharp dresser. He had on a cowboy hat, a pair of tennis shoes, a black bow tie and was smoking a Sherlock Holmes pipe.) He looked at Henry, spread his tail feathers and said, "I own this farm. I bought it from the bank, so walk around me you numbskull kid or I'll chase you clear to New York City."

"Better leave that turkey alone, "I hollered. "Or

149

he'll fightcha."

"Ain't no dumb turkey gonna bluff me," Henry said. For once, he showed good sense. He walked around Tom and climbed up on the wagon seat.

We drove past the chicken coop as a hen cackled to let the world know she had laid an egg. Grandma waved as the wagon rattled past the house. The mules settled into a steady walk. Heel chains on their tugs jingled a happy tune. A meadow lark called.

We unloaded tools and tied the mules to the back of the wagon. "Hey," Henry said. "I'll flip ya ta see who digs the new postholes." I lost and set to work digging holes while Henry moved the barbed wire back out of the way.

"Rats," I said. "Here comes Elmer Tillitson." Elmer didn't like me. Every chance he had he'd tell me, and anyone within earshot, how dumb and stupid I was.

Henry waved and said, "Good morning, Mr. Tillitson. I hope you're having a fine day, sir."
Sometimes I'd like to knock Henry's block off. The way he "yes sirred" and "no sirred" Elmer every time he saw him made me wanna 'puke'.

"Good ta see ya, Henry." Elmer said. "What ya doin' out here on this fence with that brainless Oris?" Elmer glared at me with a look that would take the paint off the side of a barn.

"Sir, I'm staying with the Fletchers while my folks are gone up to Montana for the summer. Mr. Fletcher sent me over here to repair this fence."

"You're a good boy, Henry. More 'n I can say 'bout that idiot over there tryin' ta digga posthole," Elmer said. He glared at me again.

Henry waved as Elmer gunned his old 1928 Model A Ford pickup and departed in a cloud of dust.

I leaned the posthole digger against the fence and walked to the wagon to get a drink of water from the canvas water bag. "Henry, you make me downright sick the way you always butter up that old stinker."

"Just 'cause he don't like you don't make him a bad guy."

"You know as well as I do, he's nothing but a foul-tempered ol' billy goat," I said.

We removed the old posts, set new ones, and tightened the five wires. "Come on, let's take a break before we head back to the barn," Henry said.

"Sounds good to me."

We stood in the welcome shade of a majestic old cottonwood tree. Henry put a Lucky Strike between his lips. He scratched a match on the zipper of his Levis, lit the cigarette, and took a deep drag. He blew smoke like he'd been smoking all his life. (He couldn't inhale yet without coughing up his socks.) "Do you reckon your Grandad would take us into town this evening so we can go to the show? The new show *Skudda Ho, Scudda Hey* opened last night. I'd like to see it. It's about a team of mules. You'd like it 'cause you ain't got any better sense than to like mules."

"We could ask him. No you ask him," I said. "You're so full of crap it makes you better than me at asking."

"Okay. I'll ask him."

The entire time we were cleaning the chicken coop I had to listen to Henry talk about which girl in town liked him the best—which one had the prettiest eyes—which one had the prettiest hair.

We helped Grandad do the evening chores. Henry picked the right minute to ask Grandad if he'd take us to town after supper. "Mr. Fletcher, Oris wants me to ask if you'll take us to town tonight so we can go to the show?"

Grandad scratched his nose, smiled, and said, "Ya mean ya ain't tired after workin' all day? Ya still got 'nough energy ta go runnin' 'round ta night?" After a few seconds of cemetery-dead silence, a smile appeared around the corners of his mouth. "I suppose I can do that, but you'll hafta git a ride home."

"Thank you, Mr. Fletcher. We'll catch a ride home and be up early tomorrow morning ready for a full day's work," Henry said, all smooth and polite.

After supper, I helped Grandma with the dishes while Henry got ready.

"You boys should be going to bed early tonight," Grandma said, "instead of running around late when you have to work tomorrow. Don't go getting into mischief. You hear?"

Grandad dropped us off in front of the Rialto Theater. Ramon, Marvin, and Jerry were standing by the curb watching girls walk by. All five of us wore white T-shirts with sleeves rolled to the top of our shoulders, starched Levis with a sharp crease ironed in them, and penny loafers. We had everything under control. Ramon passed around a pack of Lucky Strikes. Henry had a pack of Lucky Strikes rolled in the left sleeve of his T-shirt. No way in heck would he unroll that sleeve. He might not get it rolled up just right again and wouldn't look all tough and important. (He made a big show of striking a match on his belt buckle and holding the match for the guys to light their smokes.)

A new shiny 1948 black Buick stopped in front of the theater and deposited three girls on the sidewalk. Henry and Ramon checked them over. (They acted like they had never seen girls before.) The blonde, a new girl in town, glanced at Henry. Right-there-on-the-spot, he fell in love and looked like someone had hit him in the head with a hammer. This was a normal reaction for Henry. If a pretty girl accidentally looked at him, he was convinced she couldn't live without him. And, he 'knew' he couldn't live without her.

After the show let out, Ramon dropped us off at the crossroads. We were going to walk to Grandad's from there. The night was warm. A full moon bathed the area in a brilliant silver light. As we walked along the road, Henry was unusually quiet. All of a sudden, he stopped and said, "That foxy blonde likes me."

"You gotta be out of your mind," I said. "She never once looked at you. You're so stupid you stink. Not every girl in this hick town is in love with you. Come to think about it, I don't know of one single, solitary girl that even likes you."

"What do you know anyway?" Henry said. "You're too ugly and bashful to even look at a girl."

We turned the corner. Elmer's farm was on our right. We walked down the road, and Challenger, Elmer's prize two-year-old Guernsey bull, followed along with us inside his pasture fence. Challenger stopped and said, "Where you men going on this warm summer night? You guys let me out. I'm bored and need to see something other than the inside of this pasture."

Henry looked at me. I looked at him. Neither of us said a word. I crawled through the fence. Removing my belt, I ran it through Challenger's nose ring so I could lead him. Henry opened the gate. Challenger followed me out onto the road. Henry closed the gate and caught up with me and Challenger. One Guernsey bull and two teenage boys heading east enjoying the bright moon light and a warm summer night.

"Oris, what we gonna do with this darn bull?"

"Don't know," I said. "But we gotta do somethin' with him to cause ol' ferret-face Elmer a world of worry."

Henry laughed and said, "Sounds like a plan. I can see that old buzzard tomorrow morning when he finds his bull gone. What we gonna do if a car comes along? I don't wanna get caught out here on this road with a stolen bull. We'd probably end up in jail for five hundred years."

"Don't worry," I said. "If we meet a car, we'll turn the other way. If they ask what's going on, I'll tell 'em we found Elmer's bull out and we're takin' 'im home."

"I'm glad it's you and not me leading this dumb bull," Henry said. "I don't like the way he's looking at us."

"He won't hurt ya, ya little sissy."

"I don't care. He's a bull and they can be meaner 'n fresh cat crap."

Challenger, leading like a pet dog, didn't give us a lick of trouble. He acted like strolling down a country road was something he did every night.

"I got an idea," I said. "Let's put this guy in the old hay shed south of Leroy's place. Grandad said Leroy and his family won't be back for another week." Leroy lived about a half mile east of Elmer. The shed was a good 500 feet from other farm buildings.

Henry laughed and said, "Good idea. I shoulda thought of that myself."

"Man. You can't think of anything. Your mind's too cluttered thinking you're God's gift to women."

"Ya know somethin', Oris? You're a first-class horse's rear end."

"You autta know. It takes one to know one."

The bull stopped, looked at Henry and said, "Are girls the only thing you can think about, and talk about, and dream about? I got news for you, kid. You're still a little puppy. Those girls don't even know you're on the same planet. Forget about them. Get me off this road and out of sight and don't take all night about it. Ya hear?" (Henry wasn't used to a bull telling him the truth, let alone what to do.)

We stopped at the watering trough to let Challenger drink. While he was drinking, Henry looked in the shop to see if he could find a tub or half-barrel to take to the shed.

"Hey, Oris, I found a big ol' tub. You take that bull down to the shed, and I'll bring the tub. Then I'll pack some water to it."

"Okay. I'll see if I can find some hay for him."

I put three flakes of hay in the corner of the shed. Henry filled the tub with water. "That should keep this guy happy and quiet until we can get over here tomorrow night and feed him again," I said.

We scratched Challenger on the neck, turned him loose, and closed the gate. He looked at us and said, "Thanks, guys. I'll be okay here until you get back tomorrow. I reckon ol' Elmer will have a litter of kittens when he finds me gone come sunrise."

Pleased with the inspired prank we had pulled on Elmer, we shook hands and congratulated one another with a pat on the back.

We opened the door to Grandma's kitchen as the mantle clock in the living room struck 1:00 a.m.

At breakfast, as Grandma put three fluffy buttermilk pancakes on Henry's plate, she said to him, "Your Aunt Martha called while you boys were at the show last night. She will pick you up right after supper tonight and take you with her to visit your Grandad. You will stay with her so you can move some boxes in the garage. She will have you back here the next morning. I told her we would be finished with supper by 6:30."

Henry looked at Grandad and said, "Mr. Fletcher. I was looking forward to helping you. I hate to leave you in a lurch, but guess I'd better go with my aunt."

"That's okay, Henry. Oris can help with what needs ta be done 'til ya get back. I 'preciate ya helpin' out."

Henry and I were putting in place a new gate Grandad had built for the corral when we heard a car coming fast up the lane. Standing by the gate post with a hammer in his right hand, Grandad said, "Somethin's chewin' on Elmer. He's drivin' like the mill tails o' hell are bite'n him where he sets. Hope he stops his ol' clunker before he hits this here new gate."

Brakes squealed. Tires slid. Dust billowed. Elmer hopped out of the car leaving the door open and engine running. "Ben," he said. "My bull's gone! He ain't in his pasture. Gate's shut. No way could he git out! You seen 'im? I been lookin' for 'im since daylight. None of the neighbors have seen him. No way could that bull jist fly over a fence. I tell ya! Somethin' ain't right here. Ya reckon somebody stole 'im? There's not a better bull anywhere. Lots o' folks would like ta have 'im."

"Hold on there," Grandad said. "Ain't no one gone 'n stole yer bull, Elmer. Ya know as well as me, cows are always gitten out. They always show up. No cows been stole here since the depression. Yer bull'll show up."

"I hope so. Keep yer eye out fer 'im and let me know if ya see 'im. I'm goin' over by Earl's ta see if he's seen 'im. I got other things that need doin' besides lookin' fer a bull."

Henry and I leaned against the pole corral and listened to Grandad and Elmer. We turned and looked the other way before Elmer or Grandad saw the sparkle in our eyes and the smile on our lips. Seein' Elmer all stewed up did us good.

Grandad watched Elmer drive off down the road. "Don't know as I ever seen Elmer so worked up. He shore sets store by Challenger. It's kinda funny, that bull gittin' out. Fence is horse-high, hog-tight, and bull-strong. Beats the tar outta me how he got hisself out."

The morning wore on. Grandad had a slew of

things he needed us to do. (Just before noon, Grandad's stomach asked him if his throat had been cut.) "Well, boys," he said. "Let's go ta the house and see what we can find ta eat. I don't know 'bout you, but I'm hungry 'nough ta eat an old shoe that's been boiled fer awhile."

Grandma had gone to town. She left a note on the kitchen table. "Dinner's in the warming oven. Fresh apple pie in the pantry. Put your dirty dishes in the sink."

After dinner, Henry and I mucked out the calf pen, repaired some fence, split wood, hitched mules to the wagon, and hauled two loads of trash and dumped it in the gully east of the barn. By then, it was time to do evening chores.

Henry straddled a calf's neck, trying to teach it to drink milk from a small bucket.

"Oris," Grandad said. "When you boys finish feedin' them hungry calves, call itta day. I'm gonna check on ol' Pansy and see if the stork has brung her a baby calf yet."

The calf Henry was feeding butted the bucket from his hand. Henry slipped and went sprawling across the floor ending up on his stomach in a pool of warm, sticky milk. He tried to stand up. The floor was slick. He slipped again and fell in warm milk. He wasn't happy. After a couple of slippery tries, he got on his feet, kicked the bucket against the wall and stormed out the door, leaving me to finish feeding the calves.

(Henry wasn't use to wallowing in warm, wet milk.)

By the time I had finished feeding calves and got to the house, Henry had washed up and was sitting on the back step. "Hey, Pantywaist," I jeered. "What are you doing sitting there looking like a little baby who lost his sugar-tit."

"I'll sugar-tit you, you horse's butt!"

"WOW! I'm so scared I'm shaking!"

Grandma called us to come in and eat supper. "Come on, Henry," I said. "Let's eat."

"I don't wanna eat. All I want to do is get off this darn farm and as far away from your sorry butt as I can get!"

While we ate, Henry sat on the porch step and sulked like a spoiled brat. His aunt came to get him. She visited with Grandma. Henry sat in her car and continued to sulk. As they drove out of the driveway, he rolled down the window and hollered at me. "Sure as God made billy goats, I'll get you, and you'll be sorry, you ugly horse's butt! Wait and see!"

I stood in the yard and watched the taillights on the car until they disappeared around the bend. I went back in the house with a smile on my face. "What ya smilin' 'bout, Oris?" Grandad asked.

"You shoulda seen Henry sprawled on that floor in a puddle of milk. He was so mad smoke came out of his ears." I laughed.

Grandma gave me that what's-wrong-with-you

look. Then, she proceeded to tell me what a fine young man Henry was, and how lucky I was to have him for a friend. She went on for several minutes. (It was all I could do to keep from laughing right out loud.)

The next morning at breakfast, as I was trying to get on the outside of a stack of fluffy buttermilk pancakes, Grandad said, "Oris, I want ya ta hitch Buck and Jack ta the small wagon and go over ta Earl's and git twenty cedar posts. When ya git back, we'll fix some fence along the ditch east of the barn."

"Okay," I said.

When I arrived at Earl's, he opened the gate and told me to drive to the barn and load the fence posts while he changed the water in his wife's vegetable garden. He said I would have them loaded by the time he'd finished changing the water.

Every farm wife in the neighborhood had a vegetable garden. Earl's wife raised a small productive garden and reigned supreme at the county fair. Her vegetables always placed first in the exhibits. Every year Grandma Fletcher entered her best pumpkin and butternut squash, only to have Earl's wife walk off with the coveted blue ribbon. Her pumpkin always grew larger and the butternut squash had a better shape.

I watched Earl change the water on the pumpkin rows. Now, I knew why Earl's wife won the coveted blue ribbons. Earl wasn't too good to do women's work—he irrigated his wife's garden. I decided I'd tease Grandad Fletcher by telling him the reason Earl's wife won the blue ribbons. Grandad did a lot of chores to help Grandma, but he drew the line at irrigating her garden.

Grandad was always teasing me. Now was my chance to get back at him.

The day grew into a long one. By dinner time, I had dug nine post holes and set a new cedar post in each. Grandad figured a boy should keep busy and not sit around. I cleaned and straightened up the shop, hauled and spread 11 wheelbarrow loads of chicken manure on the garden, and helped Grandma pull weeds.

"You wanna keep doin' women's work pullin' weeds, or do ya wanna help me do chores?" Grandad asked, and he laughed.

"Maybe if you did a little women's work and watered Grandma's garden her pumpkins and butternut squash would be as big and shapely as Mrs. Brooks'." I looked up at Grandad waiting for an answer.

Grandad, with a twinkle in his eyes, scratched his nose and said, "Boy. Are you tryin' ta git me in trouble?"

"Go on you two, and get out of my way," Grandma said. "Wish I could go hide in the barn like you're going to. But someone has to work around here." She smiled.

By the time chores were finished, night was chasing

the last rays of sunlight behind the mountain.

I slid into my chair at the supper table.

"Are you hungry?" Grandma asked.

"Yes, ma'am."

"Wonder why Henry ain't back yet?" Grandad said. "Thought he was comin' back sometime this mornin'."

"Grandpa. When Henry pitches a snit-fit, it usually takes a couple of days for him to quit acting like a spoiled baby."

Grandma scowled at me over her glasses and said, "Now, Oris. That's not a nice thing to say about Henry. He's a very sensitive young man, and he's your friend."

A car drove into the yard saving me from a lecture I knew was coming. Grandma's attention turned to clearing the supper dishes off the table. Grandad winked at me as he pushed his chair back.

Mom, with the fury of an Arkansas tornado, burst into the kitchen! Dad right behind her. From the look on her face, I knew I was in a 'heap of trouble.' (I'd seen that look before.) She stared at me for a few seconds while she found her voice. I looked to Dad for help. No help there.

"Do you lay awake at night thinking of ways to embarrass your father and me? I don't know what to do with you! Elmer came by late this afternoon. He was fit to be tied, and I don't blame him! What on earth were you thinking? Again, you weren't thinking. What possessed you to hide his bull? People in the

163

neighborhood spent time looking for that bull. Time they didn't have to spare. Elmer saw Henry at the hardware store. Henry told him you took that bull over to Leroy's shed and left him there. Henry said he wanted nothing to do with the joke. He walked off and left you, and you pulled that sick prank!"

Dad got into the picture. "Oris. You caused a lot of trouble and worry for Elmer and everyone in the neighborhood. After Elmer calmed down, I told him you'd work for him free one day a week for the rest of the summer. Now what da you have ta say for yourself?"

I looked at the floor and said, "I don't know."

Mom hit the roof. "If that kid says 'I don't know' one more time, I'll scream!"

Grandma looked at me. Her sad eyes told me I'd disappointed her. Mom, still breathing fire, glared at me. It didn't take a rocket scientist to know Dad wanted to skin me alive. Granddad scratched his nose and winked at me. The left corner of his mouth twitched a little.

Those days working for Elmer were the worst days of my life. No matter how hard I tried, I couldn't do a thing to please him and every five minutes he'd let me know it.

Summer eased along. Henry got over his snit-fit. We were best friends again.

From the Author

This man by the side of the road influenced my whole life. I never forgot the fear of my first comprehension of war, or my understanding of the pain this man had experienced. At the tender age of 8 years old, I grew up, just enough to realize life wasn't always about riding Red, driving the cart, and doing chores I *didn't want to do*. I realized for the first time that life was about doing what was required even if I *didn't want to do it*.

The man by the side of the road is about a way of life dealing with the trials that come our way. It's a kind of knowing that we must take the next step not because we have a place to go, but simply because the next step is what comes after all the places we've been.

I learned that growing up really is not optional.

About Oris George—

Oris George lives in Colorado, a little closer to the river than he'd probably like, with a few more birds than he wants to listen to, and more often than not, he would rather be working with mules, donkeys, dogs, or kids.

His memories are peppered with enchanting stories picked up along the Back Roads through years of yesterday. His unique style of taking readers along the paths of boyhood adventures, days long past, and the gentler times we all wish we could once again experience, brings out the child in each of us. Capers only a young boy, a mule, a donkey, a dog, and friends could endure vanished along with the era of lemonade on the porch and Grandma's home-baked cookies on Friday afternoon.

The nostalgia that brings these summers back for a lingering glance, a memory, and a flash of experience appears in each of his short stories.

These essays will be published in various forms, including occasional blog posts and on his website. You'll want to read each and every story to be certain you don't miss a lesson, an experience, or the grand humor of a boy growing up in a time when birds still chirped, clouds still drifted across clear blue skies, and the only thing that disrupted a young boy's childhood was nightly chores and Mama calling.

For more information about Oris George, visit his website at <u>www.OrisGeorge.com</u>.

Afterward

The heart never lies… and other fallacies of youth will come tumbling back to mind as you read these stories by one of the world's simplest authors. You'll choke back tears of recognition as you read through the *Man at the Side of the Road*. You'll laugh when you read about Red the mule dumping Mule-Apples in the eggs and on Oris' head. And… You will stare off in wonder at the innocence that has escaped us over the past 75 years of living.

Fireflies dancing in the darkness, bumble bees flitting from flower to flower, and donkeys and mules meandering across the pasture, share no secrets with little boys playing at the treasure of living as want-to-be men full grown. Time does not stand still in the hills as boys attempt to learn the lessons life shared, through the experiences of growing up. Stories that reveal these details of adventures, had in the good days of yore and yesterday, don't give away the secrets. They simply revel in the joy of living.

Before God made computers, He made pencils. If you go by the George home on any given Writer's Night, you'll be seated before a roaring fire, provided a comfy chair, a cozy cup of the most delectable hot chocolate, plenty of paper and a pencil. Yes, a pencil. Because when you're at the Oris George home, it's like stepping back in time to those cozy, comfortable days that passed long ago… *along the back roads of yesterday.*

~Jan Verhoeff

Unfamiliar Words & Phrases (Glossary)

As you read the stories inside this book, you may come across a few words or phrases that are unfamiliar to you. These words and phrases are not uncommon in some areas, but in others are totally unheard of. I've gathered a list of unlikely words and phrases to help you understand each of the stories in this book.

The Man at the Side of the Road

Driving to cart.....A mule or horse hitched to a cart going down the road.

Walking Staff.....Walking or hiking with a single walking staff or pole can give an extra point of stability.

Little Man

Leg Up.....Help someone mount a horse or mule.

Home Comfort cookstove.....Beautifully made wood-burning kitchen stove. The Cadillac of cookstoves.

Heat grill.....A grill mounted in the floor which

enabled heat from the rooms below to flow upward in a multi-story house.

Stove lid.....A cover mounted in the top of a wood-burning cookstove. Usually cast iron and can become very hot very quickly.

Ol Sam, a Mule

Percheron.....An extremely large breed of draft horse known for their willingness to work, musculature and intelligence. They were originally bred as war horses.

Mammoth Jack.....An extremely large donkey standing at least 14 hands high (56 inches).

Kansas Chief.....A world famous Mammoth Jack around 1916.

Feed alley.....The alley in front of horse stalls.

Mule Apples!

Rhode Island Red hen.....A breed of chicken originally bred in Rhode Island. Known for their bright red color. Layers of large brown eggs.

Candled eggs.....Process of determining whether or not an egg has been fertilized or has a spot in the egg.. The eggs were passed in front of a candle in a darkened room or in a box to keep extraneous light from shining on the egg. Fertilized eggs are preferred by some people, not preferred by other people. Fertilized eggs are popular in health food circles.

Studebaker cart.....A horse/mule-drawn cart built by the Studebaker Company before they started producing automobiles.

White Leghorn.....Prolific layer of white eggs.

Speck inside the egg.....An egg which has been fertilized will show a speck inside it in the candling process. Also, a bloody speck will show.
Cow-hocked.....A condition in which the rear legs of an animal appear bent inward at the knees. Causes painful walking in most animals.

A Perfect Understanding

Spring Wagon......Old time horse/mule-drawn wagon, so called because it had springs running across the width under the wagon bed, giving a softer ride.

Mammoth Jennet…..A female of the Mammoth Jack breed.

Hands…..4 inches, the average hand width used to measure the height of a mule or horse without using a tape measure. 14 hands high. 14hh (56 inches tall at the withers). 16 hh (64 inches tall at the withers).

Palomino…..A particular color pattern of a mule/horse consisting of a gold-colored body with white mane and tail.

Snuffy Smith…..Hillbilly character in the comic strip 'Barney Google.'

Jenny…..A female donkey.

Attila the Hun…..Attila is generally acknowledged as the cruel leader of the Huns who conquered most of Europe from Eurasia during the 5th century A.D.

Fox Trot…..A four-beat diagonal gait in which the horse/mule appears to walk with its front legs and trot with its hind. The gait, however, is not a mixed patter of footfalls, it has a clear pattern of diagonal foot movement where the front foot hits the ground split-second before the opposite rear foot. The head shakes in unison with the rhythm of the gait. The tail perfectly balances the movements of the head. Because the animal has a four-beat motion rather than a two-beat trot, the gait produces a smooth, comfortable ride. It is accompanied by an up and down head nodding.

Gaited.....the ability of a gait, usually between 10-17 mph.

Ol' Blue and Charlie

Trace chains.....The chains, eight links, on the end of two heavy straps connecting a horse/mule to the vehicle it is pulling.

Hame.....One of the two curved metal or wooden pieces of a harness to which the tugs or trace chains are connected.

End gate.....The wooden equivalent of a tailgate on a horse cart.

Collar pad.....A pad which goes underneath a horse or mule's collar which keeps the collar from rubbing its skin raw.

ORIS GEORGE

A Man Full-Grown and His Donkey

Sam Hill…..Euphemism for hell.

4-H…..A youth organization administered by a sub-division of the USDA. At this time it was an agriculturally focused organization.

Bull Durham…..A particularly hot-burning shredded tobacco leaf produced in a cotton pouch for roll-your-own cigarettes.

Buffaloed…..Bewildered, faked out.

Hitch ring…..A steel ring (usually mounted on a post) for tying a horse/mule.

Blue roan…..A donkey with white hairs intermingled with a black base color, except in the mane, tail, head and legs.

Mower knife…. A long knife with numerous sharp individual sections used in a Horse drawn mower to cut hay.

Ball peen hammer…..A blacksmith's hammer with a flat face on one side and a hemispherical face on the opposite.

Head gate.....A control gate which controls the flow of water in an irrigation ditch.

#2 irrigating shovel.....A spade-shaped shovel used for flood irrigation. Sometimes half of the blade length is cut away keeping the original shape, making it easier to handle the weight of the mud in the ditch.

Faded Blue Bonnet

V-2 Rocket.....A large liquid-fueled missile developed and used during WW2 by Nazi Germany.

Slip.....A small implement used to move dirt pulled by mules/horses.

Fresno.....An implement used to move dirt pulled by mules/horses.

Span of Mules.....Two mules hitched together.

Feed Straw.....When hay is in short supply, it was possible to feed mules straw. Straw can be a good energy source for draft animals, but it is extremely low in protein for them.

Help in the Hay.....The process of converting the

various types of hay into a storable supply of food for farm animals.

Sounds Like a Plan

Scratched a match on my pant leg…..Denim pants were made of much coarser material in the past. A strike-anywhere match could be lit on a pant leg because of the heat generated.

Rockford pocket watch…..A beautifully made pocket watch produced by the Rockford watch company between 1876 and 1915. Approximately one million watches were made by this company.

Elmer's Bull

Bains wagon…..A buckboard-style wagon produced in Kenosha, Wisconsin.

Heel chains….. The chains, eight links, on the end of two heavy straps connecting a horse/mule to the vehicle or farm implement they are pulling.

Tugs / traces….Long heavy leather straps or chains that connect a horse/mule to the vehicle or farm implement they are pulling.

Canvas water bag…..A water bag made of canvas which keeps water cool through evaporation.

Five wires….Five single strands of barbed wire fencing.

Nose ring…..A steel or copper ring installed through the nose of a farm animal to give control of the animal.

Mill tails o'hell…..A mill tail is the water flowing after passing through a water-powered mill. You can figure out the rest.

Mucked out…..Cleaned out calf droppings and soiled bedding straw. A real sh!@#y job.

Pantywaist…..At the time, a particularly vile thing to call your friend.

Sugar-tit…..Cloth tied around a bit of sugar to serve as a pacifier; before pacifiers were invented, if you can believe it.

Cedar post…..Western red cedar provides some of the best fence post material in the world. It will outlast steel posts by more than 20 years.

Changed the water…..Changed the flow of water in a garden or crop field from one row to another to ensure all plants are provided adequate water.